FATHERS

OF

EDENVILLE

CORRINE ARDOIN

Black Rose Writing | Texas

ISBN: 978-1-68433-453-7
PUBLISHED BY BLACK ROSE WRITING
www.blackrosewriting.com

Printed in the United States of America
Suggested Retail Price (SRP) $18.95

Fathers of Edenville is printed in Garamond

*As a planet-friendly publisher, Black Rose Writing does its best to
eliminate unnecessary waste to reduce paper usage and energy
costs, while never compromising the reading experience. As a result,
the final word count vs. page count may not meet common
expectations.

*This book is dedicated to my husband, Dan, and to our sons, Ira and Ian,
for all their love, encouragement, and support.*

FATHERS

OF

EDENVILLE

PROLOGUE

At twelve years of age, he wanted to be like his father, but he was not. His dad was a composer of great poems, a wordsmith of uncanny exactness. Reveling in yet another snippet of beauty secreted away in a small, black box, he knew this to be true.

No one was around. He hurried over to the bookshelf, where his father quietly placed the box. Picking it up, he felt its rough smoothness in his hands, while carrying it to the small table beside his father's chair. Once he sat down, he recalled one Sunday afternoon. Rich, savory smells drifted from the kitchen that day. His mother cooked chicken and dumplings, quietly humming to herself, busily preparing their meal. Tromping across the crackling linoleum in her black oxfords, she stepped out of the kitchen to check on him.

"Tucker James? What are you up to?"

Quickly, he peeked in the box and drew out what had been written, before hurriedly returning it to its hiding place.

His father wrote, "Never waits the dawn when love is new and tender. It awakens yet like steeds of Ancient Rome that pull their golden chariot 'cross the dome of blue above. The dome of the world, its missive cast each day as trumpets blare! Heed their cry! The song triumphantly sweet, their truth oft times sad and ponderous. Night cannot be reached from such lofty worlds. It is death and darkness to this blissful height where only does this love exist in light, in radiant joy. Where two may yet be one again, may death then be life's enduring hope. Death is life's mystery. The sun, its fateful messenger, lends passage to the night through what must yet be lived. Now, it waits alone, this love that once knew not of time. It lived but in a moment death has made forever still, grief's yearning for the one. Whose voice, whose touch may only carry to the heights such wretched pain it struck, the arrow deep? The dawn's enraptured by love's song, where truths arise, borne upon life's tragedies." It was signed, "Tucker Howard Stewart, Edenville, 1947."

CHAPTER ONE

Her gloved fingers could not feel the rough, cool bricks as she strummed their mossy surface. Carefully moving along the narrow alleyway, she sidestepped tumbled piles of brick and old lumber, so as not to scuff her Sunday shoes. An Easter suit, made of fine-knit fabric, she wore to church that morning. Skirt and jacket, with matching, pale-peach-colored hat, the kind she had seen early film stars wear, completed her ensemble. The stockings she wore were not silk, but she cared for them as though they were the finest.

The storm pushed onward. Tall stacks of clouds passed overhead, the sun weakening, low in the gray-streaked horizon. Dirt and grass, muddy and damp, eluded her watchful eyes quickly checking behind one last time. The end of the alley was reached and, before her, lay the muddy, puddled road. Across, stood the roadside trees the sun's last glinting light played amongst. Beyond these . . . freedom.

Sylvia was her name, not born to riches or even the comfort of having only to ask for what she needed. Her life of thirty years, thirty-one in May, had been spent erasing her past. She often told herself it was what she worked very hard to overcome. A Catholic upbringing reminded her of continual temptations of which she would always be faced and knew well. It stressed the need to pray to Almighty God for forgiveness of her sins, and this she did nightly.

Her mother died when she was only nine years of age. Due to her having overcome this difficulty, she often corrected herself, saying she was much older at the time. Her father, not present in the landscape of her memories, merely faded out of existence. It was the grief of her mother's passing that caused him to go to bed one day and "never get back up," as Aunt Justice, who then raised Sylvia, often remarked in behind-the-hand whispers.

Sylvia also overcame this, her father sitting on the edge of the bed, springs scraping and squeaking. His hands hung clasped between his knees where he stared at the floor. She watched him through the hinged opening from behind the door of her room, looking beyond the painted wood hallway, at his unshaven, uncombed, unbathed, and unlaundered form. When friends took to slyly passing him unlabeled bottles at the back of the church, which he tucked beneath his work coat, Aunt Justice came for her.

Low voices conversed in another room. Her father gave her a strange hug she barely felt. He took her three dresses, her socks, panties, and undershirts, folded and placed them neatly in a brown night case that belonged to her mother. No longer entering what had been he and his wife's bedroom, he retreated to the spare room and took up his grievous duty of fading away.

Aunt Justice, named at birth by her late father upon his release from the county jail, took Sylvia's light touch of a hand into her own and bore her away from that house of grief and sorrow. Hearing her father's faint goodbye coming from the doorway behind, Sylvia refused to turn and acknowledge his presence. In that moment, she overcame her own grief, whispering to herself, pledging a solemn vow, "I'm not sad and I'm not sorry."

Sylvia stepped across the muddy road, looking around to assure herself no one was to be seen. The wind was blowing and she grew chill. She hurried lightly down the well-worn path in weeds and undergrowth, mere ragged forms in the early spring barrenness and gloom. It was not far before the trees and bushes hid her from sight of the road, unaware she was not completely out-of-view of watchful eyes. She neglected to consider someone might be in those closed shops and offices she stole past from within their shielding shadows.

A man, her husband's friend no more, since they had been rivals for Sylvia's once-youthful attentions, saw everything. Well, he saw enough. Hands in the pockets of his workday slacks, shirt unbuttoned, and curiosity bringing a slight grin and furrowed brow to his puzzled face, he stood at the window, second floor of the office where he worked. During the week, he operated the printing press for the small town's newspaper, proudly continuing his father's and grandfather's legacy. But this was Sunday and it was Easter. Earlier in the day, he decided to wander over and check up on things. It was but one moment when he stood to stretch and swing his arms about, look out the window to study the clouds, one moment chosen as Sylvia passed beneath, across the road and into the trees.

He shook his head, scratched an area behind his neck that did not itch, and ran his fingers through his hair and across his rough jaw. Dropping back into his creaking, wooden office chair, attempts to continue working were useless. It no longer held his interest. In his good-natured way, he admitted the only purpose it served was to occupy his time on a free Sunday afternoon. He had a lot of free Sunday afternoons. Now, he looked neither forward to who-knows-what, in the form of food or entertainment, nor to his darkening office.

Reaching for the lamp chain, he recalled almost with a sense of relief, the power had gone out on Friday. The storm knocked a tree down across an electrical line workers had yet to finish repairing. He sprung out of his chair like a fidgety schoolboy given permission to leave class early. It rolled away unnoticed across the warped wooden floor. Lifting his coat and hat from the coatrack, he surveyed the room to make sure nothing was forgotten. Descending the well-worn stairs, he was soon out the door.

After locking it, he turned the knob to be sure it was secure. Checking his pocket watch, he looked across to the trees and spotted Sylvia's footprints visible in the mud. They led from the alleyway to the path in the weeds. He recalled seeing her in church, standing beside her husband, as "Faith of Our Fathers" was sung. It was sung every Sunday morning after communion, before the priest's parting words. Observing her, he witnessed a momentary glance from beneath her down-swept hat brim. Directed across the center aisle, her eyes briefly settled upon what's-his-name, Jim—he dared not recall the last name—Hart. Tucker no longer derived amusement from Sylvia's behavior. Only pure, overwhelming concern motivated him to act. Without hesitation, without questioning his own behavior, he followed the same path to the other side of the trees. From there, he entered an open field, spying a distant house with one lantern lit in a back room.

What bothered him was, this man, a no-good, shady character, in his opinion, bore the same name as himself. He long ago tried to distinguish himself from Jim Hart by correcting people, telling them to call him, "Tucker," like his father. By the end of high school, nearly everyone who knew him had grown used to calling him, "Jim." His father was Tucker Howard Stewart. He was Tucker James Stewart, named after the film star, a man he could neither emulate nor ever bear a likeness.

Upon reaching the house, he saw silhouettes move across the lit window, thinly veiled before his peering eyes. He braced himself for a closer look. A dog barked. Tucker watched as it hurriedly dashed through the tall weeds and overgrown hedges. He caught himself, shocked and in disbelief over what he intended to do. Quickly leaning back against the building's peeling, crackling paint, he tried to think what he should do. They were talking inside, so he strained to listen.

Jim's voice suddenly yelled, "I don't know any more than you do! All right?! She's nuts! *Nuts!*"

A German Shepherd burst through the broken slats of an old fence and rushed up to Tucker. Pinned to the wall in the last light of evening, the dog's gruff barks alerted everyone to his presence.

Jim came outside and stood leaning over the fence. He tried to figure out why the dog was barking, calling out, "Shep! Shep!"

Another voice, which Tucker recognized as that of the man's wife, questioned, "What's going on, Jim?" She stood by, as Tucker gave up and strode through the weeds toward where they held their ground, looking puzzled and worried.

Jim's face lit up in recognition, "Oh! Hey! It's Jim Stewart, from the newspaper," and blurted out a short-lived burst of nervous laughter.

It was dampened immediately by his wife's stern look, directed at Tucker. Jim merely stood beside her saying nothing, while she followed Tucker's every move.

Her pinned hair, in his imagination, was flying loose like flames or the snakes of Medusa. She held her arms folded firmly across the extensive rolls of her midsection, apparently ignoring his fabricated explanation.

"I was out for a walk . . . tried to take a short-cut home . . . got caught out in the dark . . . I ought to know better."

Clambering over their toppled-down fence, he broke through the slats, apologizing repeatedly. Stepping in the dog's mess on the other side of the fence, he saw the expression on the woman's face remain unchanged. It was like that of a wide-eyed owl. He further imagined her nose as its sharply hooked bill.

Walking hurriedly away down their drive, he paused from time to time to scrape the bottom of his shoe in the grass, before stopping to take one last look around in the near-darkness. Jim and his wife returned to their house, so Tucker relaxed, relieved that unfortunate encounter was over. Continuing on his way, a burdensome heaviness suddenly poured over him. He felt very tired. Going over in his mind what he saw earlier, he kept shaking his head, baffled he did not see one sign of Sylvia.

CHAPTER TWO

The darkness drew in deeper beneath the trees. Night settled into the forest as Tucker walked home. Turning his head sharply toward every rustle or swish of leaves, he thanked God when he finally stepped onto the main road. Other lantern lights glowed softly and grew in number. Gone was the uneasiness beginning the moment he saw Sylvia looking at another man in church. He allowed for this welcomed sense of relief rather than admit he planned to forget the whole evening. He believed he made a fool of himself and to the one man he loathed having witness this fact.

Jim Hart was popular in their high school days. A proud young man, before years in an unhappy marriage, and never getting ahead in life, wore it away. He was captain of the football team and at the center of every girl's attention. Handsome, with dark, wavy hair, he was described as a *"dream"* by all the swooning glances never looking Tucker's way.

Tucker believed he deserved to be captain of the football team. He wished he was at the center of every girl's attention, or, at least, one girl's in particular. Why Sylvia avoided him back then, especially after—it was an unsolved mystery to him, one that yet lived and drove him—

He knew Sylvia's house was coming up and guessed it was her on the porch of their dark home. The fiery tip of a cigarette moved up through the air and grew more fiery. He grudgingly admitted being curious, probably to the point of obsession—he never went out at night—and decided to ask her outright what she had been doing. After all, he reminded himself, they were practically next-door neighbors. They were on friendly enough terms, he continued to rationalize, even if her bulldog of a husband hovered over her whenever he came near.

Her husband, Fortuitous Sumner—everyone called him Fort Sumner, Forty, or worse, when they were kids—sometime back when he was a child, developed a habit of plugging his navel with the tip of his middle finger and this habit grew, along with his stomach, into a nervous tugging.

Tucker decided to let the whole evening settle away into forgetfulness, to keep walking past and pretend he failed to notice Sylvia, but refused to let it go. Once he placed his foot on their porch steps, Fortuitous stood up from a darker area previously hiding him from view. Tucker could tell by the movement of his arm and clearing of his throat, Forty had a hold of his navel and was tugging away at it.

"Looking for something, Jim?"

"No, I was out checking around the neighborhood to see if the power line was getting taken care of—"

"You can see for yourself, it hasn't."

"Yes, you're right." With good-nights and see-you-laters, Tucker reluctantly proceeded homeward, thoroughly embarrassed and frustrated.

Walking home, he began to wonder why someone as pretty and intelligent as Sylvia married a man like Fortuitous Sumner. Mulling over what he saw as faults, there was, first of all, Forty's hair. He combed it with grease, to flatten it. It had a tendency to spring back up, sometimes unexpectedly, which Tucker found endlessly amusing. It was neither blond nor red. Tucker tried to remember what that color of hair was called, remembering words like strawberry-blond and dishwater-blond. His mother called his own hair-color an "indifferent-brown," which he supposed meant she was displeased with him, and his hair. Forty's habit of running his fingertips across the surface of his stomach, eventually finding his navel, Tucker always found strange. He forgot when it began, though believed it most likely related to some sort of childhood insecurity.

Admittedly, Forty was not the only one with an odd habit. Tucker remembered what his father used to do while reading the newspaper, one leg always dramatically placed over the other. His eyebrows raised as he scanned over the pages, occasionally shaking them into submission until they stood up straight. He twitched his upper lip and quickly squeezed his eyes shut and opened them up again real fast. He said he disagreed with someone's opinion, therefore needed to adjust his face after having his intelligence insulted in such a manner. His father once said Sylvia's hair was as black as a raven's wing, her eyes gray as smoke. An image of her drifting up out of a chimney and toward the stars, appeared in Tucker's mind, and he smiled.

His pleasant reverie faded fast once he thought of Jim Hart. Tucker forgot how much he disliked him. Jim never used any hair grease. Although, Tucker laughed in remembrance of one incident in high school. He caught Jim in the locker room one day, sprinkling cologne, or something or other, onto his comb.

Dragging it through his hair made it shiny and smell like his grandmother's herb garden, which she proudly called her "spaghetti garden." Especially funny to Tucker, when he asked Jim if that was something he needed to use for lice, and caught the look on his face, eyes squinting and jaws tightening.

Stopping at his house, he tried to make out the time. Too dark to read his pocket watch, he sighed heavily. He glanced over at the door, not yet ready to go inside.

"Probably not much warmer than out here," he said.

He hosed off his one befouled shoe. Disgusted, he dared not consider what the Hart's were feeding their dog that smelled so over-boiled. At last, sitting on the steps to his porch, he indulged in his obsession.

He saw Sylvia take the path into the trees. It only led in one direction, straight over to Jim's place and, yet, she was gone. Pondering whether she reached his house, Tucker recalled Jim's angry voice declaring, "She's nuts!" Various possible scenarios came to mind. But, in his struggle to know what happened to Sylvia, nothing satisfied his need to uncover the truth.

After a while longer, reluctant to enter his too-quiet and too-cold house, he scanned through his mind, seeking other, more serious events in his life. Eventually, he settled on one, the death of his mother. His brother, Dewey, wrote her a letter that arrived in the mail earlier that day. He saw her reading it while seated at the kitchen table, handkerchief at the ready. He asked to go over to play with Sylvia, but she did not answer, so he silently snuck out the door. Deciding to play at the school, he began to run down the street, when his mother yelled, "Tucker James! Tucker James!"

When she called his name in such a way, it only meant one thing. Grandpa needing tending. A whole variety of things his grandpa needed help doing, were pointedly shouted out by his mother. Mostly, he needed help tying his shoes, untying his shoes, finding his glasses, or cleaning his glasses. Long-faced, Tucker carried out each order. His grandpa grumbled and griped. One of his hands wobbled and shook uncontrollably. The other whacked him good with a folded newspaper if Tucker failed to precisely follow every dreaded order.

Stalling out in the yard, his name was called again. He dawdled and peeked around the trunk of the tree his mother swore he was still too small to climb. Over on the wash porch, she was busy snapping and whipping the creases out of each wet article of clothing she ran through the wringer. She filled a basketful and hefted it. Grunting, she quickly set it down again, rubbing the lower part of her back.

"Tucker James Stewart!!"

Now, she was mad! Tucker came running. His mother picked up the basket again and carried it over to the clothesline. He slowed to a walk as she set the basket down and rubbed her back again, saw her stare at him with eyes fixed. She stood frozen in position. He stopped and watched her drop to her knees and topple over. After raising eight children, his mother died right before his eyes.

The doctor, according to his best friend, Sylvia Cadwallader, said his mother's heart had given up the ghost, which sounded terrible to a ten-year-old boy. Yet, now a grown man of thirty-two, that ghost still haunted him. He lingered awhile longer on his porch, despite the growing chill, which caused his hands to stiffen and his back to ache. Also hungry, he knew he needed to eventually go inside. He looked over toward Sylvia's house, puzzling over what happened to her.

He went over the sequence of events from the beginning. Sylvia looked across the aisle in church with this appealing sadness to her eyes. When he saw it was Jim for whom she evidently pined, Tucker wished he looked the other way and missed seeing anything. He did see, and the same, tired feeling he felt earlier settled in on him again, as the events of that day played on like a moving picture he kept on viewing. Each scene took him meandering further, wandering slowly into the past.

Sometime after church, he left his house and walked toward the newspaper office. He felt an impulse to take action, walking to the office to check up on things, concerned, because someone might be lurking within the damp shadows of the aged structures. The sunlight broke through the clouds, filtering down through the tall, wind-blown elms in softly radiant streams of light. He reveled at the sight. At the back of his mind, appeared a face, a single glance not meant for him.

Once at the office, he saw no one, not outside the building, not inside, yet his uneasiness, his sense of someone there, did not yield to the fact. A story the editor asked him to write for the paper, sat on his desk, unfinished. It represented his latest attempt as a columnist for the paper, in addition to running the press. He checked his pocket watch, sat down to work, and immediately began to daydream. The weather was too extraordinary, the day too special, and his life too important to bother with an insignificant newspaper column on a Sunday. In truth, a woman's yearning gaze kept him rooted in his chair, repeatedly checking the time.

After going over the sequence of his own actions, Tucker admonished himself, no longer able to deny what drove him to behave so impulsively. He admitted he followed Sylvia. But, he was unwilling to see he felt envious of Jim Hart. Lowering his head down to his knees drawn up close to his chest, he wrapped his arms around them and around what he had no idea, as yet, were his unmet needs, his unheeded yearning. Unfortunately, one more piece of evidence had yet to claim his guilt. He was not prepared to face it.

CHAPTER THREE

Sylvia remained seated in the dark. A man's work coat draped her shoulders. It belonged to her father, but she forgot how or when it came to be in her possession. A thick, gritty smell of grease and gasoline permeated it, odors rich and deep in its fabric, as if it had been laying in the back of a truck for a very long time. She wrapped it tighter around herself. Ignoring her husband, he eventually went inside to stumble through the dark, looking for a flashlight or candles.

She laid her head back against the cushioned chair in which she was sitting. Its brown, coarse-stitched upholstery bore the signs of age, torn and musty from mildew, spotted with many stains upon stains. They told the story of its long-forgotten origin, her childhood home. Her eyes pooled with tears unable to overcome their barriers. Smoke from her cigarette, burning away in the ashtray on the porch railing, carried her sight inward.

Seeking her most-private thoughts, she visited a special memory, the time when she and Tucker became more than best friends. They played together every day when they were children. Upon entering her teens, something began to change in her, made plainly and uncomfortably evident when she first started high school. She saw him through different eyes. No longer was he the boy with whom she played. He became tall over the summer, two years ahead of her in school. The first time she saw him on campus, he said hello to her. Confident and athletic, he looked at her, up and down with his eyes, grinning and behaving in such a manner she thought was absolutely silly. Annoyed, she avoided him. Thereafter, she associated only with people her own age and those Aunt Justice pre-approved. Nevertheless, he made constant attempts to attract her attention, rushing to hold a door open for her, calling out her name in a sing-song way, waving at her when she did look at him. Yet, despite all his attention, it was Fortuitous Sumner, whom her aunt pre-approved, Tucker's friend-turned-rival, whom she welcomed into their home every Sunday afternoon for supper.

She pretended to dislike Tucker's attention, noticing her the way he did. She would suppress a smile and turn away toward her group of friends as though to resume a conversation. But, she was unable to deny how she felt when he was near her. Certain that it was temptation speaking, not love, she believed it signaled a warning she must try harder to avoid him. This decision proved impossible to heed. One day, in the autumn of her sophomore year, she stayed after school, volunteering to help one of her teachers. On her way home, she ran into Tucker, also barely leaving the school. His big grin, upon seeing her, told her how pleased he was, as he hurried up to walk beside her.

When she said, "Hello, Jim," he told her not to call him, "Jim," anymore, said he wanted everyone to call him, "Tucker." She agreed and, though they continued slowly walking along together, side by side, Sylvia found herself unable to think of anything to say. She began missing the easy, close friendship they shared as children.

She looked at him walking alongside, recalling when she last felt close to him, like they were in a world of their own, always together. It was the day he kissed her. Failing to notice the feelings coming over her as she unconsciously admired him, temptation rose up unchallenged and as bright and fiery as the leaves blowing down, like silent bursts of flame.

He began telling her all about his latest big achievement in football, of which he experienced a lot, she observed. He was very excited, humorously acting-out for her all the play-by-play details. Before Sylvia knew it, they were laughing together, enjoying one another. After awhile, they came to a bend in the road where there were no houses in view. No one could see them together, or so she thought. What happened next was so determined and wild, it seemed she only realized what happened several years later, when she found herself married to Fortuitous Sumner. Not until then, did she venture, only in secret, to reflect upon that one time, the first and last time she spent with Tucker as something more than friends.

When she arrived at home that day, her aunt seemed to read her mind the moment she walked into the house. Aunt Justice's eyes narrowed and her fists settled themselves on her wide hips, angrily looking on through the screen door, as Tucker stepped jauntily toward his own home.

She remarked, "That Stewart boy! *Whistling* as pleased as can be!"

Eyes glowering at Sylvia, her finger pointed up the stairs, sending Sylvia to her room where she was to beg for the Lord's forgiveness.

Even though it became well known to everyone, she was to eventually marry Forty Sumner, she secretly carried on with other boys, even grown men, as she had done with Tucker. She developed her own habit, falling into temptation, thankful for the freedom she felt, going straight to Purgatory afterward. She lay in bed at night, crying with her hand covering her mouth so her aunt would not hear.

Sound has other ways of manifesting itself. Her aunt heard clearly when she saw how men looked at her, noticing the comments they made. Mentioning it at dinner one evening, going on and on how she disapproved of Sylvia's behavior, Aunt Justice openly accused her of encouraging these men. Ruthlessly condemning her niece, Sylvia lowered her head and cried into her napkin. Forty informed her aunt he also heard what people in town were saying. He sat across the dinner table from Sylvia, summoning his courage to save her from herself, he assured her and her aunt. While buttering a roll, he very kindly asked her to marry him, an offer her aunt later advised she had better accept, or else.

Jim Hart was a different matter. Thinking of him drew her deeper into herself, to the memory of their first time together at his parent's house, so very long ago. Ever since then, they met with one another from time to time. She always liked him. She felt attracted to something about him, which she thought they shared, whether an unspoken agreement or an understanding. She believed she loved him and that he experienced the same feelings of love and devotion toward her. Contrary to what she told her aunt, when reminded of her vows immediately after she and Forty's wedding, Sylvia may have forsaken all other men, but she never gave up Jim Hart.

• • •

Still sitting outside, Tucker finally admitted why he felt uneasy that day, because he witnessed Sylvia looking at Jim. Her behavior was far from new. Everyone, he saw for himself, looked the other way for years, pretending not to notice. Tucker noticed. His uneasiness, his unshakeable restlessness, is what led him to head down to the office on Easter Sunday, so he could check up on things.

His behavior appalled him. He spied on her! It was not quite like that, he rationalized. He hoped she would pass by again. He saw her run across the road before, taking the path through the trees, at the same time of day. How he knew this was the most difficult for him to admit. He felt ashamed. Nevertheless, by this point, he was equally obsessed with understanding his own behavior as he was Sylvia's. Like a guilt-ridden man on trial facing criminal charges, Tucker looked straight out into the darkness of the night and admitted, not only did he know when to expect Sylvia, but when to look out the window for her. He knew this, because he habitually looked at his watch every time in the past he saw her. It was true. He walked to the office, sat at his desk, kept track of the time, waiting for the precise moment when Sylvia crossed the road. When she did, he hurried after her, because—

He remembered, on one occasion, he saw Forty walking past the newspaper office shortly after seeing Sylvia. Someone else in the office told him Forty asked to talk to him. This last time he saw her, it was only moments later when he left the office to follow her, not registering the fact there was another man standing at a distance. It was Fortuitous Sumner! Forty watched the whole thing! Tucker covered his face with his hands, in horror, dragging them downward as he moaned, shocked at his carelessness. His stomach growled and his back grew stiff. His mouth was dry and sour. The cold air chilled his neck and his hands, so he lifted the collar on his coat and buried his hands deep within its pockets. Fortuitous, his long-time rival, believed something was going on between him and Sylvia. Tucker often wished it was so, but it was not.

CHAPTER FOUR

Fortuitous Sumner stood in the middle of the road earlier that day, spotting Sylvia, and his rival following her. A friend tipped him off and, now, Forty believed he witnessed it for himself. Tucker Stewart and his wife were romantically involved with one another! Forty began to plan his next course of action. Eager for revenge, he appealed to the heavens, beseeching what he called the Lord's vindictive wrath. Emboldened, he announced aloud, "I'm not going to be made a fool of by that sneaking pansy!" Engaging in his nervous habit, he decided to bring up the matter with his wife. Hurrying along, he prayed extra hard for what he long ago surmised was Sylvia's tortured, wayward soul.

When Sylvia finally returned home, Forty waited for her by the door, watching her walk across the yard. He noted she still wore her Easter outfit. He looked at her muddy shoes, then at her disheveled hair. The light was too dim for him to see her face. After she entered the house, he slowly closed the door, leaving them in the dark. She remained by his side as he turned and stood behind her, placing his hands lightly about her waist. In almost a whisper, he directed her forward, saying, "Come on, sweetheart.

It's time to go upstairs." He moved her along up the long flight of stairs and down the hall until they were in their bedroom. He shut the door and Sylvia began to pray.

Forty had his eye on Tucker for some time. He closely followed his and Sylvia's behavior. Suspicious of them, when Sylvia looked across the aisle in church, he believed she looked at Tucker. Later, he saw them hurry off into the trees. By that evening, when his neighbor set foot on their porch, Forty was furious! Afterward, he confronted his wife, but she told him nothing. He struggled to understand why she refused to come clean on her involvement with Tucker Stewart.

Growing impatient with her silence, Forty sprung into action, whispering to himself, "The Lord's private eye has been called to duty!"

He told Sylvia he needed to look for a flashlight and candles. Secretly, he hunted for an old derringer he found and to which someone gave him cartridges. Soon, she came in, lit a lantern, and told him she was going to bed. He dismissed her with the assertion she treated the whole matter like some kind of joke.

Determined to prove his innocence, Tucker marched over to Forty's house. He planned to face him and talk openly concerning what took place. They were once friends. He believed their recent run-in with one another presented an opportunity to finally resolve their differences. Even though he knew it was unlikely, he strode confidently up the road.

When he approached their house, seeing no one outside, he proceeded up the steps to the front door. It was wide open. The interior of the house was almost completely dark. Drawers were pulled open, then slammed closed, hinges creaked, and cupboard doors banged. He heard the shuffling of shoes and Forty's angry and bitter voice, mumbling. A flashlight shone, randomly shooting its weakening beam around the rooms and along the walls. Forty was looking for something. Tucker quickly backed away from the doorway and hurriedly retreated.

"Definitely the wrong time to visit," he told himself.

Reluctantly, he began to leave. After a few paces, he hesitated. Turning to look back, he casually glanced over the house's aged and weathered form. Fixing his gaze upon an upstairs front window, he beheld a lantern. It lent its golden light from behind a curtain. The moon's light broke through the clouded sky and shone upon the house momentarily, but soon withdrew into obscurity.

Unable to find the gun, Forty assumed Sylvia hid it from him. Mocking what she said before, he repeated aloud to himself in a high-pitched voice, "Why do you want to save that piece of junk? It probably doesn't even work anymore." He was desperate to find that gun. Whispering to himself, he plotted, "I'll take care of Sylvia first, then head out the back door and over to Stewart's, put him in his rightful place. No one makes a fool out of Fortuitous Sumner. No, sir. I've got to make things right, make them pay. 'An eye for an eye,' saith the Lord." He went out to the back porch and impatiently yelled out, "Where is that damn gun?!"

Finally, he discovered the small derringer. It was in a cardboard box full of old junk next to the trash can. Somehow, it looked bigger than he remembered. One thought of Tucker touching his wife and he quickly reached down and snatched up the gun. Dashing back up the steps, he flung open the screen door, nearly tripping over the threshold upon entering the house.

Tucker could hear Fortuitous stomping around, going up the stairs, and calling Sylvia. He saw the darting light from the flashlight through the upstairs windows. Listening awhile, he saw the light again, jumping around, Forty going downstairs. The back door slammed shut with a loud bang. Tucker's heart began to pound violently. He rushed to hide behind a tree. Leaning out from around the trunk, he saw the flashlight shining in the alley, presuming it to be Forty walking behind the row of houses. The light went out and, cursing, Forty whacked it a few times. The flashlight came back on, so he continued on his way, almost at a run.

Tucker wondered where Forty might be going. Without thinking, he hurried into their house, slowly feeling his way up the stairs, then along the hallway. His heart pounded rapidly, but seemed to jerk to a stop when he thought he heard a car backfire somewhere in the neighborhood. Resuming his search, he quietly and carefully felt his way along the walls of the hallway until he came to a door that moved, having only been ajar. He opened it further. Listening intently, he strained his eyes to make out any shapes, when the overhead light came on, the power restored!

Stunned at first, he quickly glanced around the room. It was a bedroom used for storage, only a dusty, brass bed frame propped against one wall and a few scattered stacks of boxes in the middle of the floor. Curious, he looked inside one box. It contained a collection of Detective's Digest, Forty's obsession. Intrigued, Tucker browsed through the small magazines, grinning and quietly chuckling over some of the titles on the covers, like *Lee Harvey Oswald Meets the Invisible Man*. *Precinct 57*. *A Night on the Town with Nick Silver*. *How To Be a Detective In 30 Days*.

Hurrying down the alley, gun in hand, Forty tripped over a rock protruding through the dirt and fell. Surprisingly, the gun went off. Cussing out of humiliation, he knew he shot himself, though unsure where the bullet hit. Several areas felt painful, maybe only scraped and bruised, he hoped. The flashlight was also dropped. He felt around for it on his hands and knees. Finding it, he banged it a few times. Once the lights in the neighborhood came back on, he merely threw it aside in disgust. A siren peeled through the night, wailing louder and louder. Unaware it had anything to do with him, he struggled to get up, picked up the gun, and limped his way over to a brighter area in the alley to check and see where he was bleeding.

The squalling siren grew louder. He feared someone called the sheriff on him, figuring it was probably the old woman who lived in the corner house. Before he turned to hobble his way home, a sheriff's car swung into the alley. Its bright headlights glared in Forty's face. Covering his eyes with gun in hand, he unwittingly betrayed his guilt. Convincing himself there was nothing to fear, he practiced telling the officer to help him go after Tucker. He imagined being Detective Matt Harworth in *Lulu's Revenge,* one of his detective stories. Harworth enlisted the aid of the Evanstown police when they found him breaking into Lulu's apartment. They were grateful to him. Lulu picked up men at the bar and lured them to her place, killing them and later dumping the body.

"Freeze!"

With car headlights shining, the deputy stood behind the opened door, his gun aimed at Forty. Realizing who it was, he relaxed into a slump and shook his head. He wasted his time chasing after Forty out playing detective again.

"Set the gun down, Forty."

Fortuitous was not giving up. He shouted to the officer what he rehearsed in his mind, "Bob! You showed up just in time!"

Bob rolled his eyes and took a deep sigh, put his gun in his holster, and walked tiredly over to Forty. Holding out his hand, he demanded, "All right, Fort, give me the gun and we'll go down to the station and talk this over." Snapping his fingers a couple of times, he ordered him, "Come on. Hand it over." Forty began mumbling something about Harworth and someone's apartment. Bob spotted blood dripping onto the ground, coming from Forty's ear. "Forty! What did you do to yourself?!" He got him a rag to hold against his ear and drove him over to the infirmary across the highway.

Meanwhile, back at Forty's house, Tucker opened another box, abruptly brought back to reality by the sound of someone's crying. He hurried out of the room and into the hallway. Hesitating, he listened for the sound again before leaving. Another room down the hall, door closed, had to be Sylvia's. She was crying and alone, he thought, possibly in need. He stepped carefully toward her door. The crying sounds grew louder. Although Forty was still gone, he hesitated looking in on her. He should not have come into their house. Thinking to himself he should go home, he impulsively decided to talk to her. He needed to make sure she was all right. Rationalizing further, it turned into a caring, neighborly gesture.

Calling out her name, he kindly asked, "Sylvia?" Are you— are you all right?"

There was no answer.

"I—I saw your front door open and the house still dark. Anyway, I wondered if everything was okay."

Still, it was quiet.

Tucker vaguely recalled hearing a siren earlier and momentarily wondered if a house caught on fire from a kerosene lantern. Wanting to open Sylvia's bedroom door, he turned away and left their house, feeling utterly defeated.

Now that the power was back on, his life seemingly returned to normal. In his own home, with the lights on and the furnace going, he found it easy, at first, to forget his evening of impulsive and irrational behavior. Derisively laughing at himself, he placed a frozen dinner in the oven, the one with the apple cobbler. Two frozen dinners were called for, he agreed with himself, adding the turkey with stuffing and gravy, because it was Easter. His original plans for the day returned to mind. He had bought a ham. A note on the kitchen counter said to invite the librarian over for dinner. He held the paper in his hand, staring at the words, quickly folding it into his grasp. Like a basketball player on the losing team, he halfheartedly tossed the crumpled note into the trash and left the kitchen. With head hanging low, dissatisfaction filled Tucker's heart.

Stepping back into his living room, he was struck by its unfamiliarity. The peeling, yellowed walls reminded him of unopened buckets of paint stored in the shed. Spiderwebs hung from the corners in dusty, brown strands, paint raised and crackling. His old and outdated furniture never bothered him, surprisingly. It was the house coming to life and it needed a lot of work and attention.

Too exhausted to fight anymore, he sadly accepted the change in himself. He felt different, seeing things in a new way. Unaware of any reason, an explanation being unimportant, he chose to seize its momentum, take the ball and run with it, his coach used to say. Asking the librarian over for dinner was part of his old self, dusty old books and stagnation. Yet, he argued, following his original plans would have prevented him from making a fool of himself. Still, experiencing this moment, when he saw his home for the first time, he felt inspired by a renewed sense of hope. Pleased with this difference in himself, he turned on the television and plopped onto the couch.

After awhile, he got one of his meals out of the oven, leaving the other one in to continue cooking. A comedy was on television, one he missed seeing. It got him laughing and at least attempting to shake the mistakes made earlier in the evening. The hateful look on Beth's face, glaring at him as he was leaving their house, came to mind. He shuddered to think he dated her once in high school. He tried to forget that night ever since. Obviously, he failed in the endeavor.

His stomach full, the night noticeably quiet, he went to bed. Nothing further consoled him with respect to the mistakes he made that day.

"Tomorrow comes, regardless of one's failings today," he told himself.

The morning promised him a fresh start. For that, he was grateful. Letting all his final thoughts and concerns slip away, he yet felt unbearably sad. Smoke furling out of an imaginary lantern's chimney drew his attention inward, following its skyward trek onward toward the stars.

CHAPTER FIVE

Sylvia may have gone to bed, but merely lay as though asleep. Wearing only her white slip, she clutched the bible Forty handed her before he left the house. He opened the bedroom door briefly to tell her to stay put while he went outside to investigate something. "Here." He shoved his bible into her hands and left. He was very angry, almost ordering her. She feared he might do something to her should she fail to follow his order. Drawing her other hand up to her mouth, she tapped the front of her teeth repeatedly with her thumbnail. Soon, she was drifting away into her mind.

In her imagination, the slip she wore was made of genuine silk satin. A practical bridal gift from Aunt Justice, its safety-pinned straps and repaired seams gave no excuse for finery. A crystal vase, Tucker's wedding gift, drew a critical snort from her aunt. She remarked it was "ridiculous" and "typical of those Stewart's." Sylvia kept the vase filled with flowers, always in its place upon the dresser, by her side of the bed.

Her hands went limp, the bible slipping from her hand, forgotten, as she returned to her wedding day, in the summer of

1954. It began with flowers and people laughing. Everyone was so happy, talking louder than usual, excited and joyful, even giving her hugs. She marveled at the different kinds of blooms adorning her aunt's yard that morning. People gathered them from their gardens, roses of pink and yellow, delicate violets, and little, blue forget-me-nots. Garlands of yellow honeysuckle and ivy were wrapped amongst bowers and they decorated chairs and tabletops. Bunches of flowers emanated from selectively placed buckets of water.

People assembled afterward to congratulate them. She heard one woman say to her aunt, "Maybe now she'll finally straighten out."

Her aunt replied, "Well, I've done my job. It wasn't easy, either," and shook her head. Further deflecting any blame perceived to be pointing her way, she concluded, "That girl has too much of her father in her," a final judgement of which Justice was certain her listener knew well the meaning.

The talk spread to others, one man asking, "So, has Caddie sobered up, yet?" More chuckling could be heard amongst the men present.

Sylvia cried in remembrance of their comments, sobbing freely into the palms of her hands. She still felt the deep stab of pain experienced nearly thirteen years ago. Forty protectively placed his arm around her, but it was too late. Her smile had gone from the day. Arms wrapped tightly about herself, she looked around in worry. Everyone, including Forty, transformed into a crowd of unfriendly strangers. She left his side to go and pack her belongings, including a ring Jim had given her, tucking it between the folds of her handkerchiefs. Once she went downstairs and stepped out onto the porch, suitcase in hand, no one needed to tell her she was a social outcast. The early departure of guests, before the cake was even cut, including her father's absence, told her it was so. Why he did not attend what was supposed to have been her special day, Sylvia never knew. Unfortunately, it served to make the experience of ostracism all the more hurtful.

Her aunt never invited them over after the wedding and Sylvia never visited. Forty moved them into the old Cadwallader place at the furthest end of town. Far enough away from where they were raised, Sylvia decided to pretend her aunt did not exist. A few years later, her aunt was institutionalized against her will. Apparently, they found Justice wandering the new shopping center brandishing a pair of scissors. Sylvia's heart raced, swiftly placing the thought aside. She never looked at anything unpleasant or that made her feel uncomfortable. She relied on her little trick she had devised to help her to overcome all difficulties.

In her creation of reality, she felt proud of her ability to get along much better in life than others. She never drank or overate. Her cigarette smoking never developed into a habit, only something she indulged in occasionally, like when she wanted Forty to leave her alone. Years of keeping ahead of what she strived to leave behind, were adding up in her mind and in her life. Everything bothered her, not only Forty. Her choices of where to move ahead, greatly diminished. Even her mind no longer cooperated. The past edged in, despite all her efforts to hold it at bay. She strived to continue drifting away in her mind, trying to ignore the truth waiting to change her life for the better.

Forty treated her with kindness in the first several years of their marriage. Although, she knew from the start the love she felt for him, while also kind, ultimately rejected him as a husband. The only reason she stayed with him this long, rested upon the lifelong friendship they shared, which used to include Tucker Stewart.

When they were children, they played together every day. The three of them, she and Forty and Tucker, looked everywhere for money to buy candy at Forbush's Market. Before it was torn down and an apartment complex built in its place, a familiar sight in their neighborhood was the inseparable trio, each running with a sack of candy in a tight-fisted grip. They ran from the market over to Forty's house. The route they used took them around to the back of the market. A gap in the fence, where a board had been broken in two, afforded an easy escape. Squeezing through, they scrambled across the ditch, using the other half of the board as a bridge. Here, they encountered the long rows of the walnut grove. Forty lived on the other side of it.

They constructed a hideout in a thicket of trees behind his parent's house, dubbing it, "Fort Sumner," on an old piece of wood in weathered charcoal. The grass grew tallest in the shade. One of the walnut trees blew over one winter and added mystery to the area. They collected old bricks and boards, stacking them carefully to build their hideout. Besides eating candy from Forbush's Market, they playfully invented games to pass the time. Fibs were told, burping contests were held, and rumors were hatched about what grown-ups did behind closed doors. When they got older, comic books were added to the mix.

Hours were spent reading every page of every issue, including advertisements. Forty especially wanted the x-ray glasses, because he was going to be a detective someday. They needed gadgets to solve crimes. He often said, if he became a detective, he would know what went on everywhere in everyone's house. He talked about detectives so much, sometimes with his forefinger stuck in his navel, Sylvia looked away and stopped listening. Eventually, he dropped the subject. He knew Tucker also grew tired of it. He joined them less often until he stopped playing with them for good.

Curious, wanting to know what Tucker did by himself that meant more to him than comic books, Sylvia asked him one day. He rolled his eyes whenever she said something. He was almost in high school, maybe thirteen. Tightening the muscle on his arm, asking her to feel it, and showing her how fast he ran, how far he threw a ball, well, it bored Sylvia. One time, she walked away without telling him goodbye. He asked where she was going and followed her.

She stopped and demanded, "Why have you been acting so funny?"

No answer.

She shook her head and rolled her own eyes this time, giving up. They sauntered off together, slowly making their way over to her house, where Aunt Justice forbade him to enter.

Looking around at nothing in particular, he inquired in a soft-spoken sort of way, "Why doesn't your aunt let me come inside your house? It's like she hates me, or something."

Sylvia looked at the ground, thoughtful, truly wishing to know the answer herself. Shrugging her shoulders, she said, "I don't know."

Tucker said goodbye, leaning forward to kiss her, and walked away down the street. Sylvia was pleasantly surprised, but confused, her fingertips still held to her cheek. Aunt Justice scolded her for allowing such a thing. Sylvia never knew why, but her aunt disliked him, called him, "that Stewart boy," saying he was depraved, like his father. Eventually, Sylvia's visits to his house ended altogether by the start of his freshmen year. She missed him and knew he missed her. Any opportunity that presented itself, he ran to her side. She was well aware Fortuitous always watched them, at a distance, but always following them. Gone were the days running carelessly through orchards and fields. No more effortless friendships and wide-mouthed laughter revealing lost teeth and gummy blobs of taffy. Those days were gone.

Aunt Justice taught Sylvia to pray every morning and every night, before each meal and every time she had done wrong. Sylvia came to know every bead and every fragile link in her rosary necklace. When she started high school and Forty began to visit on Sundays, Aunt Justice made sure to ask if he prayed and read the bible. Sylvia learned after they were married, he prayed even more than her aunt did and would often ask Sylvia to join him every evening as he read from the bible. While not minding at first, she noticed his religious fervor grew and—

Someone was in the house! Sylvia became instantly alert. She tried to stop her crying that seemed to have been going by means of a power all its own. The boxes, in the next room down the hall, were getting moved around. A light shone from the bottom of the door. Only then, did she discover the electricity was on. Bracing herself for Forty's return, she blew out the lantern, got under the covers, and waited. He was so angry earlier, before he went out investigating. She felt around for the bible and flung it under the bed. She recalled a gun being fired and a siren following shortly thereafter. She automatically assumed trouble erupted somewhere in the neighborhood, trouble somehow connected to Forty. She was convinced—

"Sylvia?"

Sylvia held her breath in shock. It was Tucker Stewart! More surprised than frightened, she wondered what he was doing in their house and what happened to Forty. Tucker spoke to her through the closed door, his voice soothing, which she remembered from their youth, but then he left. The light went out and the floorboards creaked in the hall and down the stairs. The front door was closed and she was alone.

Hearing his kind voice, remembering she always liked that quality in him, her tears dried and her sobs quieted. She lay still and calm. A feeling awoke in her, stirring between her stomach and her chest, put to sleep long before that day. She placed her hands together over her heart. She longed to go after Tucker, to tell him what she felt for him. Sitting up, she turned on the light, reaching automatically for her rosary to quell her anxiety, but her hand reached beyond, touching the vase. The lamplight revealed to her a fine, intricate pattern etched upon its glistening surface. Swirling lines seemed to create a frame. Drawn upon the glass, a simple cottage nestled in the forest beneath a thin curl of smoke trailing upward from its chimney.

• • •

With ear bandaged and scrapes tended, Fortuitous sat quietly on the seat beside the deputy, while he was getting a ride home. Like a kid having to face his mother's scolding reproaches, he spoke not a word. He heard enough about his repeated recklessness caused by playing detective, which stifled and humbled him into silence.

Wondering why the Lord had forsaken him, he became angry and bitterly disappointed. His weight was heavy as he shifted to get comfortable. Knees, elbows, and the palms of his hands bore evidence of his humiliating failure. An old house and a barren marriage were all he had to show for years of hard work in shipping and receiving at the suitcase factory, the small town's bread and butter. With searing pain coming at him from all directions, highway reflectors and roadway signs guided the way through the night. Fortuitous became mesmerized and no longer knew himself.

He truly believed it to be his duty to bring Sylvia to salvation. It gave him a sense of purpose. It formed the basis of his marriage to her. Now, it appeared the Lord slammed that door shut in his face. He knew it closed for good and resolved to let her go. God told him loud and clear—

No, it was Nick Silver, detective extraordinaire, hat slightly tilted down to shade his cruel face, gun pointed at Fortuitous, saying, "You sorry, miserable excuse for a detective." Forty cringed on his hands and knees, exactly as he imagined the officer discovered him in the alley. Nick Silver kicked him, adding, "You're a lousy, stinkin' fool. Whatever gave you the idea you could handle a woman like Sylvia?" He shoots Forty once, twice. With blood pooling around him on the pavement, Sylvia steps out of the shadows and, together, she and Nick Silver walk away into the night.

"How's that pain medication working?"

Forty awoke from groggily dozing. He said nothing. Silence commanded him now.

Pulling up to Forty's house, Bob looked at him with genuine concern, reminding Forty, "We're gonna have to look over that gun. Can't say if and when you'll get it back. Found it, you say?"

Forty plodded blankly into his house, shut the door, and collapsed onto the sofa.

Driving away, Bob shook his head, feeling pity for Fortuitous Sumner, yet hoping this encounter was the last one involving that man.

CHAPTER SIX

Several weeks passed. Everyone involved in the evening of Easter Sunday avoided one another. Each person sank into their individual struggle. The Hart's retreated to their corner. The Sumner's suffered in their own.

Resembling a scroungy tomcat, Fortuitous' ear, ragged-edged and scarred, told everything. He steadily lost weight. Deep, dark pockets of grief developed beneath his once-bright eyes. Due to visit the doctor, he grew anxious, fearing his prescription might not be renewed. Despite being ashamed of himself, he dreaded giving up his newfound religion. While anger lurked in the corners of his mind, silence remained his master.

Having more freedom than usual, Sylvia began to worry. Fortuitous was no longer interested in her, or his navel, two things of which she oftentimes prayed to see the end. She failed to see what it meant, though tried to understand. He ate by himself, what little he did eat. His appearance bothered her greatly. Bandaged ear and a sad, weary face, only accounted for part of his irreversibly-altered demeanor. She attempted to pinpoint the cause. He carried around his vial of prescription medicine instead of his bible. Exceptional drowsiness came over him after taking his pills. When it wore off, something else took its place, keeping her at a distance.

She began to flounder in her inability to cope. She needed answers. He refused to mention that night or how he got hurt. The silence barred her from seeking an explanation, presenting an immovable barrier that came between them. It prevented her from saying anything. The reminders of something hidden deep within herself, strengthened, dredging to the surface that which she wrongly assumed did not exist. Unendurable pain emerged from those inner depths. Exposing the truth, it showed her nothing from her past was overcome.

The morning Forty was leaving to see the doctor, she held herself, pacing the floor of their bedroom. Her forehead ached. Rubbing it with her fingertips, she continued pacing. She saw him taking boxes out of the spare room and loading them in the trunk of his car. Impulsively, she hurried to the other room. The old comic books they used to read! Where did they go? He took them away!

"Forty! Some of those are mine! What are you doing?!"

Nothing she said stopped him and made him listen to her. The incident left her distraught. She stood alone in the hallway, helplessly watching Forty come up the stairs and silently walk past her on his way to their room. Their bed creaked slightly. Fearfully stepping down the hall toward their bedroom, she saw Forty's legs and feet, his hands clasped between his knees. His head slowly lowered until his palms raised to hold it.

Recklessly, without thinking of the time of day, where he might be, whether his wife was at home or at work, Sylvia fled, looking for Jim. Besieged by the present crisis, and the insistence of the past to get her attention, her movements flowed along in a dream-like state of panic. Though her habit was to turn to her current lover, a soft voice with gentle timbre called her name and she ran.

· · ·

Tucker began his vacation in a positive mood, despite his sadness. He neither wished to deny the difference in himself nor allow his life to be reduced to wallowing in self-pity. Winter's drab and gloomy presence, thus passed into memory, dismissed, for a time. Briefly admiring the day, he happily directed his attention to his chores.

He wielded the tools of his trade this morning, a clipboard and notepad. Pencil slipped behind his ear, he busily surveyed the state of his house and yard, noting everything he needed to do. He took a week off from work, because there were gutters to clean out, screens to repair, windows to scrub, and loads of weeds to pull. He smiled in pleasure, enjoying the challenge, eager to begin.

He was grateful his house was small, only one bedroom. His need for modern renovations, non-existent. Adding on rooms, he deemed unnecessary, along with redecorating and landscaping. The plague of the married man, he judged. He heeded the warnings from his co-workers who complained about these things their wives insisted on them doing. He had no use for a lawn, to be "enslaved by endless chores," quoting their words. A garden, he enjoyed immensely, though it seemed a bit hard to find in the dense growth of weeds.

He jotted down a list of what to buy at the hardware store and set out for a trip into town. A note on the counter reminded him of another task, this being Tuesday, his appointed day to visit his father. He smiled and honestly looked forward to today's visit.

An automobile was another modern convenience for which he never developed a dependency. He walked everywhere, to work, to the library, to the drugstore. When it required, he borrowed a ride home. Upon leaving his house, shopping list slipped into his back pocket, he patted the others to make sure he brought his wallet and his pocket watch. Reassured, he walked along, hoping the Sumner's were not at home.

Fortuitous drove a 1950s model Chevrolet convertible. Earlier that morning, he drove out of town to visit his doctor. It was his last visit. He ran out of his pain medication the night before and felt strangely weak. Wearing slacks not seen since his wedding day, he begrudgingly acknowledged that Sylvia always paid careful attention to their clothes. Retrieving the pants from the furthest end of his closet, he imagined them hanging in dust and spiderwebs. Surprisingly, they were neatly draped over a hanger, pressed, and smelling fresh as if only recently cleaned.

This habit was one aspect of his wife's behavior he cherished and took great pride in, especially on Sundays. When he held her arm in his and walked up to the church, he believed he was the envy of all men. Those days were over now. Though he loved his wife, an angry, brooding silence hung on and stalked him. Church, where silence reigned, became a forbidding place. Letting it go freed him to brood unobserved.

The King James bible he once proclaimed to be the Power of the Lord held in his own hand, he believed betrayed his trust. His faith, tossed into a box of Detective's Digest magazines, ruled no more.

Driving over bumps in the road, his entire collection of comic books and magazines, accumulated since childhood, bounced and shifted their weight in the trunk of his car. He planned to sell them. Although, he impulsively thought to take them to the dump. Sylvia tried to talk him out of getting rid of them. Digging through the comic books, she reminisced about Fort Sumner. Practically frantic, she begged him to let her go through them for any she might want to keep. He was disgusted with her and felt so tired. Driving along, he struggled to stay awake on the highway.

Another change he intentionally made, involved his hair. Sylvia commented he looked like a hippie, his hair uncut for months. Barely past the bottoms of his ears, Fortuitous derived satisfaction from being unconventional and rebellious. He decided to postpone cutting his hair. Checking his reflection in the rearview mirror, he wondered how he might look with a ponytail. The car swerved out of control, nearly hitting another. He snapped out of his daydreams. He remained so until he reached the doctor's office.

Sylvia fled to Jim's workplace, then to his house. Shep quietly greeted her before retreating back under the porch. Knowing that Jim was not at home, she decided to leave, when the front door swiftly flung open. His wife, Beth, stood there, angrily spewing at her for having the nerve to show up at their doorstep.

She yelled at Sylvia, "There's plenty of other men around! I'm sure one of them would be happy to take you in, you marriage wrecker!"

The door slammed and the windows shook. Shep jumped out barking, startled, and snapping. He nipped Sylvia on the leg, tearing a hole in her stockings. Beth swung the door open again and hurried to restrain him.

"Oh! Sylvia! I'm so sorry!"

Rushing to Sylvia's side, Beth's obvious, genuine concern and surprising show of pity, became the catalyst sending her plunging into her emotional wreckage. Staggering blurry-eyed, she fell toward the porch steps. Shep quickly hid under the porch when Beth hurried into the house to retrieve a first-aid kit. Crying, Sylvia pulled off her shoes and stockings.

She said whatever came to mind, "I don't know what's happened to Forty! He's been acting so strange! I don't know what to do about it! I just ran right out of the house!"

Beth thought Sylvia behaved a little overly dramatic. It confirmed in her mind the opinion many people held when it came to Sylvia Sumner, that she was a neurotic mental case. Surprising even herself, she now believed her husband's pleas of innocence.

Beth, whose name was short for, "Bethany," worked full-time as a cook at the Spring Hill Residence & Infirmary. She saw a lot over the years. Mostly, it was the elderly who tried to wander out the door. Occasionally, mentally ill and emotionally or psychologically disturbed individuals were brought in to be temporarily housed until someone from the state mental hospital came for them. Sylvia reminded her immediately of one woman who broke into hysteria every time certain kinds of men came near. The war brought in young veterans who ran down the hall, yelling, as though pursued.

The difficult part about her job was the unavoidable. It was their town's local rest home and clinic to turn to in times of need. She first started working as the rest home's kitchen helper when she dropped out of the Catholic high school at age sixteen. Her mother kicked her out of the house when one of her many boyfriends showed an overly affectionate interest in Beth. Armed with a bundle of clothes and her belongings stuffed into a grocery sack, she showed up for work one morning with no place else to go.

Jefferson Hart and his wife long felt sorry for her. They worked together at Spring Hill, he as their head cook and, she, as a registered nurse. They offered her a room in their house. She could clean and help with the children. They also advised she return to school, though she preferred attending the public high school. Through this arrangement, she met their nephew, Jim Hart, and eventually married him.

Jefferson held the title as the town's biggest gossip. He knew facts, details, and shameful secrets on nearly everybody. His mouth worked non-stop while he fried the eggs, flipped the bacon, and scraped the grill. He freely gave his opinion on everything. Beth learned over the years it was always accurate. She trusted him and his wife and, along with their children, they became her family.

Due to Jefferson Hart's constantly active mouth, Sylvia's and Tucker's family history reached Beth's ears as well. He told her about Aunt Justice "stepping off the deep end of reason" and winding up in the state mental hospital, where she died "alone and broke as an old model T." He gave her the whole story involving Sylvia's father. Jefferson described the man as "a pitiful drunk" ever since the war and his wife's death. Surprisingly, everyone in town, according to Jefferson, received the greatest shock of their lives, when Robert Cadwallader miraculously sobered up and disappeared! He even told her how Tucker's father carried on, something tragic and scandalous involving Sylvia's family.

Sadly, Uncle Jefferson ended up becoming a resident of Spring Hill after a heart attack. He died naturally and peacefully. Beth took over the position of head cook two years since. Her future felt secure, though Jefferson's widow and her assistant nurse, frequently advised Beth on other matters. Their urgent whisperings left her uneasy.

Unlike her husband's uncle, Beth did not involve herself in the comings and goings of everyone there. It was unavoidable when it came to locals. She put in her time for the day and, on her way down the front steps, encountered Tucker Stewart on his weekly visit to see his father. She avoided looking at him, regretting their embarrassingly disastrous date when they were teenagers. Angry, she mumbled he had some nerve prowling around their house. When she got home, she barely walked in the door when Sylvia showed up, acting like an abandoned puppy.

Bandaged and calmed, Sylvia's tears dried. Her shame and embarrassment poured out of her, apologizing and begging forgiveness for daring to exist, it sounded to Beth. She was moved to tears. She found it necessary to pour herself a drink. While the weeds seemed almost to be heard growing taller and the crickets sang ever louder, Sylvia and Beth talked on the porch of the ramshackle old house.

Once called Home, the neglected structure fell from grace years ago. To Beth, it was only a house. Screens were torn and the curtains were in shreds. Skunks, opossums, and mice lived underneath and within its walls. If you dropped an apple at one end of the kitchen, it rolled all the way to the other end, a downward slope. An area rug in one corner of the living room covered a hole in the floor. It no longer mattered. It was only a house.

"Well," Beth began to advise Sylvia, "you're just gonna have to talk to Forty about it, that's all."

Sylvia took a step in the wrong direction when she said, "I want to leave him and go look for my father, but I don't know where to begin."

"I'll help you!" Beth was only partially aware how eager she was to get Sylvia out of town.

Drinking the whiskey by herself, Beth believed she and Sylvia were both childless and wronged women, stuck in marriages from which neither of them knew how to extricate themselves. Even though Beth knew her own husband was at the center of their unholy predicament, she yet believed Tucker Stewart to be at fault somehow. Especially when Sylvia began to pour out her grief over the man.

She cried and said, "We used to be such good friends! I don't know what happened." Turning to Beth, she asked, "Do you know he was in our house?!"

Beth was shocked. He was even more dangerous than she earlier assumed. She asked Sylvia, "When?!"

Sylvia answered, "The night the power was out . . . Easter Sunday . . ."

"What was he doing in your house?" After it came out of her mouth, Beth imagined what he was doing and—

Sylvia continued to ramble on, "when Forty disappeared." Beth did not want to hear any more, beginning to mention what Jefferson told her about Sylvia's mother and—

Sylvia suddenly stood up and announced, "Oh! I better get home and cook my husband's dinner. I'll try talking to him. Thank-you, Beth."

Beth watched Sylvia with sad-eyed amusement, sauntering off down their driveway. It was baffling to her, this perfectly dressed woman everyone knew was the prettiest in town, walking away barefoot and bandaged.

Sylvia's shoes and stockings remained neatly set on the bottom step of the porch. Beth, her unlikely, newfound friend, went indoors to cook her own husband's dinner. Unbeknownst to herself, she once more forgave him after Sylvia's visit and, instead, wrongly pinned the blame on Tucker. She thought she knew it all. Positive he was chasing Sylvia down that one evening, she reminded herself, he was caught in the act right at their house!

Continuing to fume, she poured herself another drink. She absentmindedly returned Jim's bottle to its hiding place in a cowboy boot by the front door. She ruminated angrily over Tucker Stewart, having the nerve to go after Sylvia in her own house! It all made sense to Beth now, Sylvia running away down their drive, trying to get away from him. Recalling what Jefferson warned her about long ago, that Tucker was "a woman-chaser, just like his father," she became furious.

Fanning her blouse to cool herself, she sauntered into the kitchen. An idea popped into her head. She may have ignored Jefferson's advice back then, but now, she knew better. Things were going to be different. Spreading mustard and mayonnaise on white bread, she slapped the bologna and a sprig of lettuce between, cynically announcing dinner was served. Smiling deviously, her plot to help Sylvia leave town permanently, formulated in her mind. She was going to show that woman the door to her very own, sweet salvation.

CHAPTER SEVEN

The forested hills were cool where Tucker walked along the road overlooking the valley. Large trees grew alongside the creek below, whose leaves shimmered like round, shiny coins in the sun's morning light. The white church steeple reached toward the heavens. The reflective dome of the Catholic church bell tower, stood out amongst the trees. Elm and maple, pine and alder clustered around scattered homes and the meandering streets of his hometown. He loved one view especially. It was where he and Sylvia sat one time as children. They were excitedly pointing out their families' homes. After searching rooftops and recognizable landmarks, they shouted with joy at each discovery. His house, where he grew up, used to have a striking blue water tank behind it. That landmark was easy to find. His eldest brother lived there now, having assumed responsibility for the care of the family home. Tucker volunteered to keep a close watch on their father's care.

Walking on down the last hill, settling into the hayfields and orchards beyond, he felt a bit saddened. His brother, his father, and himself were the only ones left in what was once a large family. Two sisters lived elsewhere. He saw them very rarely, often forgetting about them. Sometimes, when he happened to remember them, it struck him, the stark realization they did not exist in his life. Their entire household was always loud, with endless activity, talking and arguing, fighting over chores and food, and room to breathe, he guessed.

Howard married, but he and his wife never had children and led very quiet lives. They rarely varied from routine, ate bland food, and always politely agreed with one another. His sister-in-law's name was, "Mary." Tucker privately called them, "Howard Hughes and Marilyn Monroe." Neither of them resembled or behaved like their namesakes. Except, Howard did keep a neatly trimmed mustache.

Heading up the steps to the rest home, Tucker spotted Beth coming out the front entrance. The glass door merely banged shut in her rush to get past him. He hardly ever saw her there. This time was especially awkward and embarrassing due to having been caught behind their house. That night was still painfully fresh in his mind. Nevertheless, he gave her a timid hello. She ignored him. Soon, she was in her car and charging out of the parking lot. Since he arrived too early, he sat down and pondered over Beth Hart.

She arrived new to their high school when they were in the early part of their junior year. He and Jim Hart had a running dare to ask her out on a date. In their locker room bantering after football practice, they talked about Beth, and Sylvia, too. While Beth was not a pretty girl like Sylvia, she was more well-endowed than any girl they had ever seen. Rumors circulated around campus. They speculated upon her mysterious past and why she came to their school. Tucker knew she lived with Jim's uncle. Even though he imagined she and Jim probably saw one another when he visited his aunt and uncle, the knowledge that Jim liked her came out much later.

It happened in their senior year, when Tucker decided to challenge their long-standing dare. He asked Beth if she wanted to have dinner with him at the town's famous chicken and rib roadhouse, "Klucky's." She said, "yes," under the condition he would also take her to the movies.

They did not have a movie theatre in their small, out-of-the-way town. Beth lived over near the high-school. Tucker knew this date involved driving. He needed to borrow a car. Nevertheless, he agreed, excited over the possibility she suggested such a thing, because she hoped they would, naturally, stop somewhere on the way home. He knew Jim would be jealous over the whole thing, so he played it up extra big in the locker room that day at school. That night turned out to be extremely humiliating for him, deservedly so, Tucker admitted. He knew it was equally as, or more humiliating for Beth, though she did not deserve it.

•   •   •

Fortuitous arrived at the doctor's office. Sitting in the waiting room, he grew impatient waiting for his name to be called. He continually got up to ask what was taking so long. At one point, a middle-aged man came in, took off his cap and sat down, gripping the bill of his hat in both hands between his legs. When the receptionist asked Fortuitous his name, the man looked up and listened intently to what was said. After Forty sat back down, the man kept looking at him. Forty expected the man to ask him something, but he remained quiet. Finally, it was Forty's turn to see the doctor and, passing by the receptionist's desk, he heard the man tell her his name.

"Cadwallader. Robert Cadwallader."

Forty flashed a look at the man and their eyes locked on one another. The man began to smile, but the receptionist asked him a question and drew his attention away. Forty was directed into another room to wait for his examination. It felt like another unbearably long wait, listening to Lawrence Welk music and thinking about the man he saw. He suspected it could be very important. The man's name, he immediately established, was definitely that of Sylvia's father. The last time Forty heard of anyone seeing him was from his own father, mentioning "that drunkard" at Klucky's roadhouse. That was years after he and Sylvia were married. He knew well the long-standing taboo of never mentioning her father ever since he put their old house up for sale.

Forty felt overburdened with the weight of its significance that, in his new life of silence, he knew not how to handle and, so, became incredibly anxious. The room turned into a box where he was held against his will. Its walls swiftly closed in on him. No windows from where he could look outside. He began counting every hinge on the door, noted any peeling paint, identified everything sitting on shelves, such as bandages, swabs, alcohol, tongue depressors—He broke out in a sweat. His hands swelled up and grew puffy until they became clammy with sweat. Thinking he might get sick or faint, he blurted out, "Why tell her something she'd only pretend she didn't hear?!"

Despite his extreme weight loss and pale, depressed appearance, Forty was given a clean bill of health by the doctor. He left the office, downcast and worried. The doctor refused to renew his prescription. By the time he was driving home, his anxiety again became overwhelming. Feeling weightless and disconnected from his surroundings, he began imagining himself a hot-air balloon. Carried away, he floated up and up into the heat of the day. Slowly leaking air, he began drifting down, down again toward the hot pavement. Whatever was happening to him was too much. He turned at a side road where he saw a park, hoping a short rest might help him to calm down and get his mind back on driving. Sitting quietly in his car beneath a shade tree, he found it impossible. He was becoming almost delirious.

All Life used to demand of him was a call to service by God and, now, he felt like its lone survivor. His trusty raft merely drifted wherever the current now carried him, no longer under his control. Trapped, caught, and unable to free himself, he panicked.

Impulsively, he got out of his car, opened the trunk, and began hauling each box over to a picnic table. It was near a group of young people, the type he called long-haired, worthless bums. One was playing a guitar. They wore their hair long and shaggy and the girls were braless. One, who was wearing a long skirt and had a small wreath of flowers in her hair, danced by herself with her eyes closed. She behaved as though the music played only in her mind. He guessed what they were up to, but uncharacteristically found it appealing. When he finished unloading the boxes, he sat on the picnic table and watched the dancing girl, the soothing medicine he craved. She stood in place, moving and swaying gently, gracefully, and effortlessly, flowing along in the wind, her arms raised and flowing with it. The music, the dancing girl, and the breeze that came up, calmed him. For the first time in weeks, he faced what happened to him and his wife. He broke down sobbing.

Face buried in his hands as his whole body shook with sobs he neglected to conceal, Fortuitous felt a nudge. He drew his hands away and they stood near him, concerned, their faces serious or worried. He never met these people. He neither knew them nor ever received such attention, such care. One of the young men had a wrinkled cigarette between his fingers, offering it to him. Though Forty knew it was not tobacco, he took it. He never smoked a day in his life, detested the fact Sylvia did, upon occasion. He attempted to smoke it anyway, holding it like he saw them holding it. He inhaled and his lungs burned raw from the smoke, coughing and sputtering. One boy took it from his hand and showed him how it was done, then gave it back to Forty, urging him to try it again.

Somewhere inside, remained a fragile speck of who he was barely two months ago. In that fragile speck he knew what he was doing, but the greater part of him no longer cared. They were passing around another one of those cigarettes, which Forty greedily took each time it came around to him. The girls were opening up the boxes and, before Forty could think why he had even brought them there, their contents were on full display. These young people were not laughing, though, like Tucker, when he found them. They were in awe, laughing with delight. Forty excitedly shared what he forgot were either going to be sold or taken to the dump.

They most especially liked the bible and, as they thumbed through pages, reading aloud to one another various passages they found, he walked away, listening to the sweetly strumming music and the boy's clear and calm voice singing. Fortuitous Sumner drove homeward in a dream-like state of euphoria, the music yet playing all around.

CHAPTER EIGHT

After her encounter with Beth Hart, Sylvia arrived at home in a daze. She managed to make it as far as the sofa. Face in a pillow, legs sprawled, she immediately settled into an oblivious, snoring slumber. The dusty soles on her feet betrayed her shoeless trek home.

Tucker left the rest home, confident his father was doing well. Attending to his shopping list occupied the remainder of his morning. Soon, bags of fertilizer, vegetables, flowers, and seeds to plant were placed outside the hardware store. He found a ride home, so Tucker checked his watch, sat on the curb, and waited.

Fortuitous came creeping along through town and parked nearby. Tucker glanced his way. Distracting himself, he examined all his newly purchased supplies, stood up, and peered into the front window of the hardware store. He looked over at Forty's car again. Resuming his inventory check, he reexamined everything he bought. Becoming impatient, he considered asking someone else for a ride home. Not ready to give up, though, he looked through the window one last time.

Seated once more along the street, Tucker propped his arms on his knees and wondered if Forty knew he was in their house that night months ago. Revisiting the moment when he stood outside Sylvia's bedroom, he recalled raising his hand, intending to knock lightly on her door. His head nearly rested upon the door panel. Sadly ashamed and disappointed in himself, he grew weary, unable to deny what followed next. He chose to face it. Why he did so, was not to torture himself with shame, but to seek understanding.

Although there were no witnesses to his actions that night, he knew that his other hand nearly touched the doorknob to Sylvia's bedroom door. Momentarily closing his eyes in regret, how much her behavior centered around his own, became clearly apparent to Tucker. Turning his head toward the other end of town, in the opposite direction of Forty's car, he scratched an itch on his back, noticing there was pain centered deep in his chest.

Forty stumbled out of his car, cursing, nearly banging the door shut on his hand. A slip of paper falling from his grasp, he failed to grab out of midair, was rapidly snatched up from the pavement. He hurried across the street, furtively darting around cars driving past. Meanwhile, behind him, his car door slowly swung open. Tucker noticed the motor was left running. He knew Forty was always very careful. He made it a point to take his keys with him and lock his car. Curious, Tucker spotted Forty's long hair immediately before he entered the drugstore.

Eager to forget his own troubles, Tucker diverted his attention to his neighbor's behavior, wanting to know the story behind his actions. More than willing to set aside his self-inquiry, the small town's busy activities effortlessly drew him out of himself. He watched people go by, driving on the street, walking past him on the sidewalk, each of them into their own thoughts, perhaps coping with their own struggles. Brief conversations started up and concluded. The laughter and loud voices of children playing at the school lifted his spirits. Business at the diner picked up and talk revolved around the daily special. It was lunchtime.

Tucker thrilled at the realization that stories were everywhere he looked. Everyone's life came together and interacted with one another in the town square. Yes, it was a small town, but it was his town, belonging to everyone he knew. It was in this place and it was spread throughout their entire valley, a rural community of homes and businesses, farms and churches.

The original town began where Tucker worked. They were the old brick buildings almost a mile south from where he sat. In addition to the printing press, there was the post office, a sculptor's studio, in what had originally been the general store, and there was a blacksmith's shop and a livery stable. It was the Hart family's long-time trade, in partnership with the Henry family. It looked abandoned, but was yet in business, although not very profitably, Tucker heard. Various wooden outbuildings and sheds stood behind the brick structures. Once called, "Pine Way," that part of town was where they all lived, the Hart's, Sylvia and Forty, and Tucker, settled in homes built in the nineteenth century. Jim and Beth Hart's house sat isolated in a field at the southwest end of their valley. Modern conveniences acquired over the years were indoor plumbing, electrical wiring, and telephones. Narrow dirt roads connected those old buildings to one another.

To Tucker, Pine Way was not only the most historical section of their town, but the most forgotten. He felt an unspoken loyalty toward the area, believing that it somehow needed each of them, personally, to survive. Though they were, for the most part, younger than those who owned homes in the more recently built areas of town, they were often called, "old-timers." Those who revered local, hometown knowledge, like Tucker, appreciated the term. Orchards, open fields, and thickets of tangled blackberry vines separated that end of town from the newer section where Tucker sat waiting.

This newer part was an attempt by those of his parent's generation to create a proper downtown where people could congregate and socialize. They often threatened to relocate the post office to this newer section, but old habits were difficult to break. People continued to drive the length of the paved road, park their cars, then walk the remaining distance to the post office, not wanting to get their cars dusty. Tucker found so many quirks such as this, which the townspeople had, he both loved them and, yes, laughed at them, though not out of ridicule, for their endearing qualities warmed his heart.

He thought of possibly writing about his observations, but words did not come easy. His father had a talent for words. He used to complain he should be writing for the paper, not printing it. Tucker never told his father he was often asked to write a piece for the newspaper. He avoided the subject. His father was a real writer, but never received credit. Now, his dad sat hunched over in a wheelchair, barely able to communicate, head nodding and one hand shaking uncontrollably. Born around 1890, he often told Tucker stories on the real old-timers who founded their town. They began the journey he proclaimed it was Tucker's responsibility to uphold.

Built in the 1920s, there was the drugstore, Goodman's hardware store, a feed store, barber shop, thrift store, the elementary school, where the public library was housed, Patty's

Beautique, and Millie's Kitchen. The diner was well-known for the best ham and bean soup made every Monday. Homes were clustered around and tucked down quiet lanes, all very straightforward and orderly. He grew up here. His family's house was on Fig Tree Lane. Next door, was the home of Sylvia's earliest childhood years, before she moved in with her aunt on Magnolia Lane, the same street where Fortuitous and his parents lived. Walnut and fruit orchards still existed in the areas to the north and south.

Past the orchards, was the newest part of town, built in the 1950s. Forbush's Market was torn down, along with the old filling station and the feed store, to accommodate the Pine Valley Marketplace. Everyone loved and hated it, because it gave so much in goods, yet added so little in character. An attempt to appease the discerning tastes of its most vocal opposition was made in the form of unique business names, like the beauty salon, "Snip it in the Bud," and the bookstore, "Read 'Em & Weep." The Hillview Apartments were nearby. The highway cut a swath along that edge of town. Klucky's dilapidated old roadhouse sat alongside it. The suitcase factory was across the highway, along with the rest home and infirmary in its sedate and very green manner. This marked the northernmost end of the valley, and of their town, known as Edenville.

Wooded hills were all around hiding and protecting their valley, like loving arms wrapped around their small bit of heaven. The high school was across the valley, over the first set of hills in the east, in a smaller valley nearly two miles away. Ever since graduating, he never returned. Its existence took place in a life apart from his own. A fairly large school, it served not only their community, but other small towns and scattered homes and ranches in a good part of the surrounding area.

Forty left the drugstore and crossed the street, shutting off his car engine and closing the door. Entering the hardware store, his appearance interrupted a loud discussion on the state of the country. Lined up along the counter, the men gathered around got one look at Forty's hair and stopped talking instantly. He was not paying any attention to them. Having found an old prescription slip in his car for pain pills, different from the ones he previously took, he changed the date on it, and managed to get it refilled. He was so relieved. Anxious to get his important errands done, he anticipated getting home and taking a couple of pills.

Tucker was getting very tired of waiting. He checked the time, deciding to see if there was someone else willing to give him a ride home. Forty came out of the hardware store, closely followed by a few other men.

One of them commented derisively, "Where you goin', old-timer? The barber's that-a-way," which started a few chuckles and more comments, like, "ain't that wife of your's feedin' you? Or, is she too busy gettin' dolled up for a night out?"

No one laughed, because Fortuitous wheeled around with the most wounded look on his face. They shrunk away and began retreating back into the store. Without thinking, Tucker hurled his own comments at the men, to which no one paid any attention.

Forty collapsed on the curb next to the sacks of fertilizer. He was hastily, and with shaky desperation, trying to pour the pain pills into his hand.

Tucker rushed over to him to stop him, as Forty greedily shoved some in his mouth. "Forty! Stop! What're you doing?!" Tucker grabbed the vial out of Forty's hand, trying to scoop up what fell in the gutter. In a quieter, calmer voice, he asked Forty,

"What's gotten into you?" He saw the ragged chunk missing from Forty's ear. "What happened?!"

Forty spilled out the contents of his sorrow, holding his head between his hands, "My wife doesn't love me! I can't stand it anymore! How's a man supposed to live like this?" He was unaware people had stopped to watch.

Tucker knew he had to do something, unable to leave him. He helped Forty into the passenger's side of his own car, sniffing the smoky air inside, "What's that smell? Have you been smoking?" He let it go and put the supplies he bought into the trunk and proceeded to drive Forty home.

Forty continued to moan and complain, bitterly lamenting his entire life's woes, "I *hate* my job! I *hated* my dad! He never let me have a dog!" He rambled on, saying, "My mom and dad fought all the time, yelling and yelling *all over the house!*" Tucker was shocked, but Forty said more, "My mom would scream and stuff would get knocked over. Then, my dad'd take her into their room." He quieted, covering his face with his hands and shaking his head, before he let his hands drop into his lap. Miserable, he tiredly added, "I can't ever get angry at Sylvia. I'm-I'm afraid what I'll do to her. I don't wanna be like my dad, that *big* galoot."

Tucker remembered Forty's meek and withdrawn mother, bruises always present and she always distant. He tried his best to focus on driving, since he was out of practice. Unexpectedly, Forty began grabbing his arm and his shirt, pleading with him, "Don't take me home, Jim! Please! Please, don't!" The car swerved every which way, veering into tall weeds to the left, then to the right, rolling haphazardly along the road.

"Okay! Okay! But—call me Tucker, all right?"

"Anything! Just don't take me home!"

Tucker agreed, but only to get Forty to stop pulling on him. He figured it might only be for a short while, at least until Forty calmed down. Soon, they arrived at Tucker's small house. He helped Forty out, got him some water, and sat him on the couch while he unloaded the trunk.

"Hey, Tucker?" Fortuitous called out for him in child-like neediness, wondering where Tucker had gone.

Tucker set everything down and went inside. He flopped back into his easy chair, after getting himself some water, and let out a loud, groaning sigh. Fortuitous was sitting there picking the scab on his ear. Next, he lightly scratched his arm, looking generally and absolutely pitiful, nothing but a hopeless, stray puppy with a bad case of fleas.

"You know what, Forty?" Tucker had the perfect idea to solve Forty's problems and cheer him up, perhaps enough to send him on his way. "Why don't we go out and find you a puppy somewhere?"

Forty's face lit up. All this in one day, he was thinking, meeting the nice young people in the park and now he was going to get a puppy! Catching himself, as though about to do wrong, he asked, "Oh . . . what would my wife say?" His mood rapidly shifted. He doubted it was possible.

Tucker refused to give up, but he knew the only puppies were at the livery stable and belonged to another one of Jim's dogs. He reminded himself, Forty had nothing against the man, evidently ignorant of the real source of his long-time jealousy and suspicions. Without considering Fortuitous might eventually uncover the truth, Tucker suggested they walk over there, maybe see if any of the pups were still left. On their way, Forty's slacks dragged the bottoms of their cuffs on the ground. He pulled them up and they slipped and sagged. Tucker was shocked at the change in Forty, thin, reminiscent of his youth, but haggard-looking despite his childish glee over getting a dog. Only vaguely did Tucker connect the pills Forty took to his behavior. Although, it reminded him of the way some people behave when drunk. It also dawned on him, not once did Forty mess with his navel.

Thankfully, Tucker thought, Jim was not at the barn. He told the blacksmith Forty wanted to have one of the puppies. Failing to notice the man reach into the stall for a specific one, he watched Forty's reaction. Forty held the little dog close to him, sitting on the hay. The frantically wiggling puppy ecstatically licked his face, whimpering excitedly. Again, Tucker was amazed. He witnessed Forty's stern and rigid demeanor melt away while holding that happy dog. Before him, was the Fortuitous Sumner he knew a very long time ago, back when comic books and candy were the only serious considerations to uphold in life.

Smelling the green, ripe odor of hay and horse manure, Tucker was reminded of when he was a child, playing in and around the barn. Lots of kids played here long ago, all the shopkeeper's children, he recalled. Drastic change appeared in their lives with the onset of war and its aftermath. His mother died. Sylvia's mother died, and she moved in with her aunt. His grandmother's spaghetti garden grew thick with weeds. One by one, his family grew smaller and smaller. He never realized until that very moment, when Forty let all the puppies climb into his lap, tugging on his shirt with their teeth, trying to lick his face, he missed those days, before the whole world changed.

Every one of his brothers, Howard, Ted, Henry, and Dewey, went to war in Europe and in the Pacific. Letters were received, each time one left home, that his mother read so often they resembled crumpled handkerchiefs whenever she held them to her face and cried. Only two of his brothers came home alive. They were Howard and Dewey. The other two, Henry and Ted, were buried one after the other in 1944 and in 1945. His mother died that year as well. His eldest sister, June, died the following year, in 1946, while giving birth to her third child who did not survive. Tucker outlived them, yet his friends were still alive and still here. This solemn bit of truth opened his eyes. He deeply and profoundly realized it was a gift he took for granted.

With Forty and his chosen pick of the litter trailing behind, they walked back to Tucker's house. The sight of Forty's car reminded him Forty was supposed to be going home. It was getting late in the day. Tucker wanted to get a start on his neglected garden. Seeing Forty playing with his puppy, he went ahead and hastily set to work pulling out the grass and spindly weeds. Whistling to the puppy, Forty gave it some water from the garden hose.

"What do I feed it, Tucker?"

"Well, you have to buy it some dog food, Forty."

"I'm gonna name her Sylvia."

Tucker coughed and laughed at the same time. "I don't think that would be a very good idea. How about Mitzy or Lady?"

"Hey, I know! I'll name her Freckles."

"Freckles?" Tucker was confused until Forty pointed out to him the spots on the puppy's face.

Reminded of Sylvia, Tucker ripped the weeds out with greater vigor. After a large pile accumulated and a wide clearing was made, he gave up and stopped for the day. With his rolled-up sleeve, he wiped the sweat from his forehead, noticing Fortuitous was not leaving like he hoped. He knew he was going to have to give him a nudge down the road back to his own house. Thinking carefully, he decided to ask Forty to go with him to buy dog food, saying the puppy was probably starved and the store was going to close soon. To his relief, Forty agreed. On their return trip, Tucker pretended to absentmindedly drive Forty to his own house.

After he got out of the car, Tucker unloaded the dog food and set it on the porch. Forty left the car door open, quietly walking toward the house, holding the puppy in his arms. Tucker wondered, either Forty was not paying attention to where he was or he no longer cared. Whichever the reason, Forty cuddled the puppy and giggled all the way into the house, leaving Tucker to sigh yet again. Picking up the dog food, he followed Fortuitous inside.

Tucker heard Sylvia vomiting in the bathroom next to the living room. He was beginning to feel ill at ease with their situation. It was only that day he and Forty's friendship had miraculously been renewed in a strange sort-of-way. Where Sylvia and himself were concerned, in his mind stirred the years of heartbreak, as well as secrecy, he was not yet ready to face. It was still too painful. Without a second thought, he left their house and walked home.

CHAPTER NINE

Standing before the mirror, Sylvia's reflection showed the flaws that lay within herself. Low, pathetic, and disgraceful, she judged, and looked away, barely able to see those two, sad eyes return her gaze. Like shadows coursing beneath awareness, dark areas and wrinkles disturbed the surface of her previously smooth face. Nausea afflicted her for the past two months. Having refused Forty's attentions for several months, perhaps as long as a year, she knew what happened. She felt nauseous again, but refused to let it take control of her. Drawing a bath, she concentrated all her effort into undressing and stepping into the bathtub without slipping.

Laying back in the tub, she closed her eyes, sinking lower into the hot water. The bathroom door lightly swung open. Its latch never worked properly. In scampered a fat, whimpering puppy. It squatted and urinated on the bathroom rug. Horrified, and happier than she felt in months, Sylvia nearly yelled, "Jim?! Is that you?!" Fortunately, she stopped herself, realizing Jim never came to her house, but—

"Come and get this dog! Look what it's done!"

Hoping and halfway-believing Jim brought the puppy, Sylvia, forgetful of her nudity, sat up in the tub, leaning over the rim when Forty ran into the bathroom. Assuming it was Jim, without looking, she expressed her joy, smiling brightly, while pointing at the rug. The puppy proceeded to drag her clothes out of the bathroom, held tightly between its teeth. Sylvia turned her head to see it was not Jim, but Forty.

In shock, Sylvia instantly yelled, "Forty! Get the dog before it does it again! My clothes!" She moaned, the nausea coming over her again, full force. She hurriedly stood up and stepped over the side of the tub, one leg still in it.

Forty hurried out, closing the door behind, as she vomited into the toilet. He chased after the puppy, already leaving numerous puddles dotted around their uncarpeted house. After quickly wiping up each one, he left and walked directly back over to Tucker's.

Sylvia finished her bath, shaking her head every so often, muttering under her breath, "It can't be the same dog. It can't be." Jim showed it to her over two months ago, saying it reminded him of her, so full of love and affection. She smiled and laughed until she cried. The sheer misery of her condition sought hope, lending her genuine happiness at the thought of Forty bringing the puppy home, her puppy. She naively considered that Jim asked him to bring it to her. Though very different than what occurred, she faithfully clung to this explanation.

Sylvia tied the sash on her oversized robe, slipping into the kitchen with the hopes of fixing a late breakfast, though wound up sitting blissfully at the kitchen table drinking coffee. Sipping and staring off into her thoughts, she reminisced about the last time she met with Jim. In the old livery stable where he worked caring for horses, he spread a blanket over the hay in the loft. They lay together before dressing, whispering softly, smiling contentedly.

That morning, after Forty left for work, Sylvia paced the floor in their house, all the while planning to meet with Jim. She fought against her sinfulness, knowing Purgatory followed without failure or forgiveness. She wanted to see him, to be free of her torturous thoughts. Trying to keep ahead, to deny them, only made it worse. Memories, unhappy, painful memories haunted her with their pleading, "Daddy? Where's Mommy? I can't find her anywhere." She held her hands over her ears as she heard again, "Daddy? I want Mommy. Where is she? Daddy? Daddy?" She tried to make it stop, even ran out of the house, into the alley behind. Holding back her tears, she walked to the livery stable, going around the buildings and coming down through the alleyway, between the newspaper office and sculptor's studio like she always did to avoid—

She tried to flee the hurtful memory of her father. Forty reminded her of him, depressed and worn out, sitting on the edge of the bed. The entire picture of her impoverished childhood overcame any remaining bastions of denial.

Sylvia missed her mother, wanting to be held in her lap, kissed and soothed. In her parent's room, where her mother may only be sleeping, cold air and dust loudly proclaimed her absence. Sylvia craved a gentle touch, a loving word. Running into the kitchen where her mother may be cooking dinner, the mess of opened jars, food left sitting out, dirty, scattered dishes, unwashed and grimy towels, and flies dancing in the air, frightened Sylvia. Dashing to her post behind her bedroom door, she watched her father. She wished and hoped for him to look for her. She imagined him raising his head to look at her, picking her up into his arms. Holding her close and kissing her with a whiskered, scratchy face that tickled, made them both laugh. Her hope fell in despair, her eyes dry and empty. Even though her father kept her fed, made sure she bathed, and took her to school and to church, he was gone.

•   •   •

Sylvia's father, Robert Cadwallader, and his new bride left the small town of Pine Way after their wedding. Prospects for work led them to a city far away, where her relatives took them in until they got themselves established. It was the summer of 1929. Hard times hit and then later worsened. He took his wife back to their hometown where Sylvia was born several years later. When the war broke out, her father longed to do his duty and, not realizing the toll it would take on them all, he kissed them goodbye, told them to be brave, and left. He was gone for three long years. Infrequent correspondences arrived postmarked from various locations around the world. Small sums of money lifted out of the envelope, her mother swiftly folded and placed in the pocket of her apron.

Sylvia listened to her mother crying nearly every night. She prayed for her father's return. Her mother's oldest sister, Aunt Justice, visited often, paying extra attention to Sylvia, eyeing her strangely, often holding onto her when Sylvia insisted she let go. Aunt Justice never found a man with whom to have children of her own. She wanted Sylvia, frequently criticizing Sylvia's mother, saying she ought to do this or that or ought not to do this or that on Sylvia's care and upbringing. Their own father, Jiminy Walker, worked, without pay, fighting on the home front while in prison. Her mother and her two aunts, Justice and Patience, never spoke of him or where he went. Sylvia learned of his whereabouts from their brother, Uncle Prosperous. He was named by their father when he found another one of his many jobs. Russ said that Grandpa Jiminy went to live in a big house and Granny Walker went with him. Sylvia sat quietly on the front steps of her aunt's house, while her uncle talked it up big with friends. She heard a lot about her whole family, more than she dared recall afterward.

Her house sat next door to Tucker's. Their mothers and his grandmother often talked and laughed, while hanging their laundry to dry or hoeing their gardens. Supposedly, her mother's gardening efforts served the purpose of directing her loving attention she would otherwise devote to her absent husband. Tucker's father often sat in a chair, reading the newspaper out on the lawn in the shade, with children playing around him. Once, when Sylvia's mother bent over in her garden, she saw him watching her. The serious expression on his face reminded her of her father when he lay on the bed watching his wife comb her dark, lustrous hair.

"She was a beauty," Tucker's father often told Sylvia.

She remembered how he acted after her mother died. He looked away, far off at nothing in particular. He gently wrapped loose strands of her hair up and over her ears, telling Sylvia she took after her mother. One time he gave her a hug, squeezed her close in his arms, and even kissed her on the head. She pointed out he had tears in his eyes, and he said, "Her's were like smoke, hair black as a raven's wing." Sylvia knew, now that she was a grown woman herself, he meant her mother.

She was only six or seven years of age. Whatever happened between her mother and Tucker's father took place in their world, not her's. Everyone kept it from her. It was secret. Upon any occasion presenting itself, he paid her visits. These so-called visits rested upon the pretense he needed to fix something or help her do something, supposedly because she had no one else. Sylvia did overhear Aunt Justice warning her mother about the danger of becoming pregnant, telling her it was sinful.

Aunt Justice stood over Sylvia's mother, their voices low in the kitchen growing more dim, even while the lights were on. Her mother sat with hands folded, silently putting up with Aunt Justice's admonitions. She was in Satan's grip, her aunt said, and the Lord would punish her. Sylvia was too young to understand. After her father finally returned, his mood changed dramatically. Oftentimes, he sat brooding, and took long walks, sometimes gone for hours. The serious talks between her mother and Aunt Justice continued, one in which her mother said she was pregnant. Confused, Sylvia wondered why they were so serious, bickering under their breath over the news.

Her mother said, "And what am I supposed to do now? Bobby will—"

Aunt Justice told her mother, "Well, you're simply going to have to let him believe it's his. And," she added with her finger wagging toward her younger sister, "thank-goodness, this didn't happen while he was overseas." Bitterly criticizing her brother-in-law, "All of this would never have happened if that husband of your's would stay put where he belonged. Going off wherever and whenever he pleases instead of staying at home *where he's needed!*" Aunt Justice was much older than her younger sisters, practically raised them, too, she often said. She got worked up, more like a scolding mother, collected her purse and gloves, then stormed out.

Sylvia found it necessary to sit on her aunt's porch steps to get the rest of the story on later days. Her Uncle Russ and his "shifty-eyed friends," as Aunt Justice referred to them, remarked how, "Yeah, that Stewart came tomcattin' around every chance he could get," which called for another drag off their home-rolled cigarettes. He also mentioned, with a sneer on his face, "And, that damn Caddie," which is what he called Sylvia's father, "can't keep his pants zipped two minutes! Home from the war, or wherever the hell he went, and he's already antsy for them foreign women! Spends a lot of time at Klucky's hopin' one'll turn up." His short-lived, yet blustery tirade, was followed by an extra big and loud hawking spit off the side of the porch, before they skedaddled out of there like a pack of stray dogs down the road.

Once, Sylvia picked up a cigarette, still burning. She held it the same way they did and sucked on one end so her cheeks caved in, the way she saw them do it. She blew out the smoke. Choking and gagging, she imitated her uncle in a raspy voice, "Stewart came tomcattin' around every chance he could get." Next, she shot out a little drip of spit, to add the needed emphasis she knew such a statement required.

Her mother's pregnancy did not go right. The baby was born as still and cold and lifeless as a soft and silken dead rabbit Sylvia once saw that a neighbor's dog killed. Her mother never laughed again. Tucker's father never looked at her again. She died before Christmas in 1945, from "grief and complications brought on by a difficult childbirth," which were the doctor's words. Sylvia did not understand many things that happened then, including something about herself. Something also grieved within her, buried so deep, it also became cold and lifeless. She became aware it stirred back to life the night Tucker entered her and Forty's house, standing outside her bedroom door, talking so nice to her.

Snapped out of her remembrances, none other than Tucker Stewart, himself, knocked at the door, wide open, as usual. He said, hello, and is anyone home. Sylvia closed her eyes, asking herself, what is happening? When is all this going to stop? When are things going to return to normal? He hesitantly walked into the house. She quickly got up from the table and began gathering up clothes to iron or wash. Uncomfortably aware she wore nothing beneath her robe, she placed the palm of her hand on her belly, bunching the fabric in her grip, before abruptly withdrawing it when Tucker spoke.

"Sylvia?" He stepped further into the house, until he stood in the kitchen with her.

"What do you want?" She refused to turn around and face him, pretending to be too busy.

The pain in his chest returned. He yearned to hold her close to him. "Forty plans to stay the night at my place. I came over to get some things he wanted me to bring to him."

"Go ahead," and still would not look at him.

He got some of the puppy food, which Sylvia noticed from the corner of her eye. He hesitated when he came back into the kitchen, merely standing in the room, waiting. Sylvia knew what he needed and went up the stairs. Tucker followed close behind, which bothered her, even to their bedroom. He stopped at the doorway. She selected a few clothing items of Forty's, noticing Tucker looking at the vase full of flowers by their bed. She pointedly stuffed the clothes onto his chest, while looking directly up into his eyes, letting him know with a glare how much he annoyed her. He grabbed them before they dropped to the floor, hurriedly moving out of her way, nearly losing his balance. Taking one more look at the vase before following her to the bathroom downstairs, he waited for her to say something. She gathered a few more items, handing him a sack in which to carry everything. In the kitchen, she drew down the ironing board from its place on the wall and set about getting her ironing done. Instantly, she was irritated, uncomfortable with him standing nearby instead of leaving.

He asked, "Mind if I get a cup of coffee?"

"Help yourself," she answered, but avoided looking at him.

He watched her, how she took great care, draping, arranging, and folding or placing on a hanger each article of clothing. It marveled him how some people knew how to do that. His father used to help his mother with the ironing.

Tucker found it unbearable, Sylvia's silent treatment and her stubborn refusal to look at him. He knew he should leave. His body refused to move. The pain that burdened his heart, grew so great in the few moments he stood helplessly watching her, he acted before he considered anything else. The moment she set the iron down, he quickly set aside the cup and went to her, took her in his arms and, with eyes closed, held her, and said, "I'm sorry, Sylvia. I'm sorry. Please, please, forgive me."

His voice, soothing and gentle, comforted Sylvia. She closed her eyes and relaxed into his arms, letting him hold her and apologize. She knew not why he apologized. He let her go as she sniffed and wiped away tears. He gathered up the sack full of Forty's belongings to take with him, turning to leave.

"Jim?" Her head turned down, then she raised it and looked directly into his eyes, "I-I mean, Tucker."

"Yes?"

"Thank-you."

Sylvia felt truly thankful for his friendship, for his kindness and love she knew he felt for her, real and honest love he gave when she had not asked.

CHAPTER TEN

Sylvia sat on the sofa, leaning forward. Her lips pulled tightly together, while her hands clasped her knees. Bare feet, one curled over the top of the other, and tired, straining eyes belied the appearance of ladylike restraint.

She casually inspected the dress she wore. Its royal-blue, nylon fabric appealed to her. The pattern of lace trim on the hem of her dress mismatched the trim on the hem of her sleeves. Merely an inexpensive dress she purchased on sale, its color brought out the gray in her eyes. Within them, reflected a clouded sky one early spring day months ago.

She checked the pin on the indigo brooch that belonged to her mother, smoothed the fabric of her dress across the tops of her thighs. Checking her hair, she deftly reined in any loose strands. Sighing impatiently, her eyes glanced down at the floor, then back out the front window. A packed overnight bag sat nearby. Beth Hart promised to drive her someplace. Sylvia made up her mind to address an important matter. Beth agreed she made the right decision. Due to arrive nearly thirty minutes ago, Sylvia sat waiting for Beth.

Friday morning threatened to break record temperatures for the month of May. Beth Hart hated hot weather. Any activity made her sweat profusely. She promised to bring Sylvia her shoes, trying to locate them, without luck. They were not in the house nor on the porch steps, so Beth immediately assumed Shep found them, imagining him chewing them into ragged bits. Although, looking under the porch, no shoes were to be seen. In the house, where she had no memory of having put them, she tried to guess where she may have absentmindedly placed them. They were nowhere. Putting off what she believed she needed to do, having lingering doubts with respect to her husband's behavior, she mentally practiced asking him if he saw a certain pair of shoes.

The very same day Sylvia forgot her shoes on their porch steps, Shep immediately picked up the stockings between his teeth. He sneaked them under the porch, wasting no time ripping them to shreds. Jim came home later that evening. He delivered a puppy out of town, along with a horse they shod. The blacksmith informed him that Forty Sumner came by earlier in the day to pick up Sylvia's puppy. By the time Jim arrived at home, he fretted whether Forty knew about himself and Sylvia, before spotting a very familiar pair of white, heeled sandals daintily set on his porch steps. He stood frozen in shock of why, how long, when, and if.

Beth's faded-yellow Chrysler sat parked in the driveway. Jim fearfully glanced toward the house, quickly snatching up the shoes. Walking hurriedly back toward his workplace, he prayed to the god of guilty, desperate men, that his wife missed seeing them. He kept checking behind to make sure she stayed in the house, while he took a hidden pathway known only to himself and to Sylvia. It remained their secret, where they waited for one another at appointed times, though not since Easter.

His wife's stinging words from that evening past, sounded once more from his memory. He counted on her cooking Easter dinner for the residents and their guests that day, but she returned home from work early. She said she felt unwell, complaining how tired she was, how sick she was, and that she needed a drink in the worst way. Jim finished his bath, standing sheepishly in front of the mirror, shaving beneath a dangling flashlight. The second time he shaved that day caught her eye, looking him up and down, before pausing to glance around the living room. He attempted cleaning house after church, an impossible task in their severely neglected home. Beth noticed what little he accomplished, the floor swept, the throw rugs straightened. He pretended not to care when she tentatively walked toward the bedroom. The only other light shone from a kerosene lantern placed on the dresser. She saw the bed, looking so neat and tidy for the first time since—She stared at it, and Jim froze, razor held in midair near his face as he looked her way, waiting.

Turning to speak to him, Beth suddenly stormed across the bedroom, shouting, "What's Sylvia doing behind our house?!"

Dropping the razor into the sink, he hurried over to the bedroom to see for himself. By then, Beth leaned out the window to yell at Sylvia standing in the field outside, looking like an injured fawn, he saw clearly. Her head lowered in shame and she slowly turned to walk away. Things turned very ugly later that night. In its aftermath, he swore to himself he would never look at Sylvia ever again. Yet, in his hand, he held her shoes.

He threw them down in disgust. Momentarily placing his hands over his face, he cried out in frustration. When he drew them away, he saw Beth standing outside, looking around at their yard, before she retreated back indoors. He aimlessly milled about beneath the trees, opening and closing his hands. Growing confused, he tightly held himself, mumbling incoherently, his chest heaving in merciless anguish perpetually riding him. From out of the dark places no one else knew, rose the awful pain Jim Hart held deep within himself. It drew him into its fold, a place of despair, images not connected to anything concrete, yet brewing and boiling in their torment. They revealed themselves, tearing him to the ground. Falling to his knees bent toward the earth, he covered his head with trembling hands fending off blows from above, sobbing and begging for the end. He remained crouched beneath the trees, gradually able to calm himself.

The song of crickets brought him back to the world. Placing one hand upon the rough bark of a tree beside him, he gradually stood up, recovering himself with a deep sigh. Unable to face his bitter, drunken wife, he quietly stepped from beneath the small grove into the moonlit night. Looking over toward his house, he saw the lights on. The television noise blared loudly. A rush of wind blew down from the forested mountainside, cooling the air and his sweaty, dusty skin. He praised the stars above, briefly hopeful. Walking away up the path to the barn, he shouted into the sculptor's studio to rouse his buddy into some hard drinking and serious forgetting. Sylvia's shoes remained scattered under the trees, where he cast them aside, and where the mountains first called to him, calling him to come home.

• • •

Sylvia sat patiently waiting at her house. In the palm of her hand she held her wedding ring. Deciding to stop waiting for Beth, she chose a different pair of shoes to wear and left. Walking around back, she unceremoniously tossed the ring into a field, determined to be done with it, taking the alleyway to a back road into town. She turned toward town at Peach Tree Lane. Stopping to visit the community cemetery, she approached one grave to pray and beseech her mother's aide. Sylvia planned to search for her father, so asked her mother for help. Jim promised her to ask if anyone he knew might know of his whereabouts. Whenever she asked him if he heard anything, he said, no. Sylvia wept over her mother's grave, recalling the last time she and Jim were together, no longer able to treasure the memory. All the while he swore to her he looked for her father, he led her up into the loft of the livery stable. It scarcely mattered Jim no longer wanted to see her, because she no longer wanted to see him.

In the mean time, Beth asked Jim if he saw a pair of shoes, describing them to him. She neglected to say to whom they belonged, so he played it safe and said, no, and left it at that. In his mind, he planned to get them the next morning. He regretted not taking them to Sylvia's house. How he wished to put an end to his misery.

Again, Beth fought with her suspicions and, grabbing a bottle of whiskey, poured herself a glassful with one hand, fanning herself with last week's mail. Not yet summer, she complained it was too hot in the house. Out on the porch, she tried fooling herself that it felt cooler, so she sat on the steps. Fanning away, she shook her head, still angry with, not her husband, but— what's-his-name. Embarrassed all over again, she recalled seeing Tucker a few days ago, irate over that night they found him behind their house, chasing after Sylvia, which she yet believed took place. She wondered how Sylvia got through their fence so easily and meant to check on it.

With glass in hand, she looked behind to see what her husband was doing. He also had a glass of whiskey in one hand, but the whole bottle in the other, sitting slouched before the television. Too drunk to notice, let alone miss her, she got up and walked along the fence line. What could hardly be called a fence anymore, lay hidden underneath and pushed over by berry vines and overgrown weeds. Together, the mess presented somewhat of a barrier, but Sylvia got through somewhere along its straight, though tangled course. An opening appeared and Beth stepped through into a small grove of pine trees. A carpet of pine needles softened her footsteps. Their scent reminded her of the best days of her youth. Before she and her husband married, he often took her to a lake in the high mountains, where pines grew in forests and their sweet fragrance filled the cool, mountain air.

This place under the pines was like the kind of hiding places she remembered favoring as a young girl, where no one could find you, not mother, not—she spotted the shoes and everything once good between her and her husband fell in ruins, not by their sight, but by the truth she had known all along. She picked them up and took them, dangling from her fingertips like they were instead a pair of dirty underwear she loathed to look upon, let alone touch, and headed directly back to their house. The second she entered it, she threw the shoes at her husband who, with glazed eyes and uncombed hair, sat up instantly, staring into his lap at Sylvia's favorite shoes. Beth stomped to the bedroom to pack. She left home quickly once before in her life and remembered how it was done.

While her husband sat with eyes closed and head down, she grabbed a grocery sack and stuffed it with anything but the clothes she wore to work. She decided to leave her "worthless, lying, cheating, and undeserving husband." Why not quit her job? She dared asked herself. One of the nurses who worked there lived miles away, in another town. She long ago offered, when Beth wised up to her husband's ways, not to hesitate to let her know. Everything packed, she drove away up the drive. Soon, she would no longer call Edenville her home. Taking the road to Sylvia's house, she plotted how to personally put an end to Sylvia's days of chasing men.

CHAPTER ELEVEN

Jim Hart sat on the worn-out old sofa he rescued from the dump years ago. His regrets gathered close, poised and ready to break his spirit. One of these clung heavily to a dangerously innocent pair of sandals, prodding him, taunting his wounded soul. Instead of returning Sylvia's shoes, he chose to go drinking, drowning himself in a bottle, because it was easier to drown than to swim.

He habitually blamed his problems in life on his father's death. Yet, creeping stealthily into his blurred awareness, arose unchallenged, the knowledge he began to drown before he finished high school, before his father died. Something within himself he fought to control, ensured his destruction.

His high school years once rejoiced in his memory. Now, they only burned. Another one of his greatest regrets was the day he chose Bethany Clark to be his girl.

They were getting to know one another, while visiting at his uncle's house, where she came to live. He caught her sneaking liquor from his uncle's makeshift bar. Uncle Jefferson set it up in his living room, a cupboard and small refrigerator salvaged from an old travel trailer. Playing bartender, he stocked it with hard liquor, mixers, and such. After work, mentioning how it was done over at Klucky's, he stood behind his homemade bar and fixed himself a drink. Jim occasionally stopped by after practice to visit. His uncle frequently handed him a glass. Jim never drank. He noticed Beth showed up in time to sweep away his glass, saving him from having to drink it, he assumed. One time, he caught sight of her in the dining room, pausing to guzzle it down on her way to the kitchen.

Before long, he connected her affectionate playfulness, not to the time they spent together, but to each untouched glass he set aside she later drank herself. He figured, as he stood watching his uncle down his first drink in one room and Beth sneak her first in another, she would outgrow it someday. Becoming uncomfortably familiar with this pattern, he began to develop his own. Quickly leaving his uncle's house, unable to bear their drinking any longer, he immediately recognized the advantage to leaving. The fun and games began.

Beth hurried outside to catch up with him. She excitedly jumped in the car, screaming and giggling, yelling, "Let's get out of here!" Witnessing this angry, anti-social girl transform into a bubbly, carefree young woman, drove him like a contagion. It was infectious. Her energy and enthusiasm for life incited his own, every time she said those words.

Sometimes, they drove all the way up into the mountains to a lake popular amongst fishermen and tourists. Other times, she pretended to help him with his homework at his own house. She tried sneaking liquor from his dad's cabinet. It bothered him, especially when she got caught there as well.

Beth's face, while plain, though not homely, appealed only to Jim, because he liked her and they were friends. Her figure, on the other hand, dominated every boy's attention. She held top status in their bawdy, locker room discussions.

Jim endeavored to become captain of the football team the following season in his senior year of high school. He aimed toward his goal and rigidly held to his path. Disciplining himself, studying hard for exams, he was determined to achieve his greatest dream, to go away to college and play college football. No other ideas or aspirations lay beyond that. This one was enough to fill him.

He played along with the locker room banter, because what he did, and often imagined doing with Beth, needed to stay in the back seat of his car. Most important, he feared his teammates might find out. They would be merciless and spread it all over school, ruining his reputation as a rising star meant for greater things. Additionally, if the coach found out, he feared getting kicked off the team. The coach strongly discouraged serious stuff with the girls, to keep their hands on the ball and their hearts on the game.

Luckily, Jim easily avoided seeing her at school, having completely different class schedules. While she took remedial courses, his teachers encouraged him to take higher-level courses. With their guidance, he worked very hard to maintain good grades. Nevertheless, his physical attraction for her grew the more often they spent time together away from school. He looked forward to seeing her. He missed her when they were apart. The secrecy gradually became a lie more painful than avoiding the one he believed he loved.

It came to an explosive conclusion at the end of football season in their senior year. Tucker announced he accepted their long-standing dare to ask Beth out on a date, and she accepted. They planned to eat dinner at Klucky's, see a movie, then—Jim failed to hear what Tucker said after that. Concealing his sudden rage instantly distracted his attention. His feelings for Beth had grown stronger. He told no one, not even Beth, because he wanted to carefully plan how it would fit in with his dream. He hoped to marry her after college. They would become engaged after graduation. Dressing in front of his open locker, he focused on his planning, for a little while. Tucker gloated shamelessly. The other teammates joined in with their raucous teasing and towel-snapping at bare bottoms, laughing over Stewart's big date with the girl with the big—

That was it for Jim. He shouted to them to shut up and strode out of the locker room, fists tightly clenched and face rigid with anger. Beth agreed to go out with Tucker, he fumed. Blaming himself, his wrath broke loose, unimpeded.

Refusing to stand by and let someone steal his girl, he went over to his uncle's house to prevent her from going, but she was gone. When his uncle handed him a drink this time, he took it. Believing he would calm down and enjoy himself once he drank, like it did for Beth, he sipped it, hating the burning, awful taste of it. He paced the floor, while his uncle observed him, shocked and concerned. Jim waited to see if the anger lessened, but it grew worse. To his horror, fear and hatred took over, weakening his self-control.

He asked his uncle for a second drink. Eyeing him, his uncle said, "No, I think one is more than enough for you," an ice cube dropping from the tongs he held, plinking into his own glass. Jim left in a hurry, with his uncle at his heels, asking, "Where are you going, Jim? What're you so mad about? Why don't you stay so we can talk it over?" Jim ignored his uncle and drove away.

He raced to Klucky's roadhouse to catch up to Tucker and Beth. Here centered his greatest regret for which neither he nor his wife granted forgiveness. He pulled into the parking area, looking for Tucker's car. While he sat in the dark and cold, thinking over what to do next, Sylvia's father, one of the regulars at the bar, came staggering outside. Jim felt sorry for Sylvia. He tried to avoid looking at him. He stood outside Jim's car window, busily digging in his pants pocket for his keys. Unfortunately, Jim saw the man bend over to vomit by the side of his Cadillac, wipe his mouth on his sleeve, urinate, then climb into the car. He passed out laying on the front seat with the headlights on.

Impatient, Jim twisted the palms of his hands gripping the steering wheel, frustrated and increasingly sickened, when Tucker and Beth came outside and walked toward an unfamiliar car. They were laughing and joking. The striking difference between their behavior together and his and Beth's when they were together, struck Jim hard. Too stunned to act, he remained in his car with one hand squeezing the door handle, staring.

As rivals, he saw Tucker as a clown and a nobody, yet he was so jealous when this clown no one took seriously, opened the car door for *his* girl, and she said, "Thank-you, Tucker," in such a ladylike manner. Without stopping to think, he acted fast, but not fast enough. Rushing to confront them, he hurriedly weaved in and around the cars parked pell mell, but Tucker drove off before he reached them. Jim pounded his fist onto the hood of another car and ran back over to his own, to hurry up and follow them. Where did this Beth come from? He asked himself. Who was she trying to fool? Jim believed he knew her best. He deemed himself the better judge of what he cynically read as her phony play-acting.

Arriving at the theater, he hastily paid for his ticket, then ran inside to look for them. The house lights went down. He sat up in the balcony, after shoving his way carelessly through a row of seats amidst pained and annoyed protests. Hoping to get a better look, he finally located them after the movie ended. The lights came on, so he pushed his way through the crowd, ignoring their angry scowls, but to no avail. Assuming Tucker and Beth got in line to buy snacks for the second movie, he lost track of them. Thinking they might have gone outside, he strode across the lobby, banged the glass door open, and stood on the sidewalk looking for them, only to see them drive past. Now, they were on their way home, he thought. He ran to his car and sped off, hoping to overtake Tucker's car and force him to pull off the highway. He was eager to fight Tucker, demand he stay away from Beth.

Coming over a rise, then heading down into their valley, he saw the rear lights of a car ahead on the highway. Thinking it had to be them, he became confused when the car pulled into Klucky's roadhouse. Skidding to a stop across the gravel parking area, he discovered it was the wrong car. Knowing it was time to give up the chase, Jim groaned in defeat, deciding to take a moment to calm down and think.

Seated in his car with the motor running, he gripped the steering wheel so hard, the palms of his hands blistered. Realizing it, he released his grasp, dropping his hands into his lap. In a moment of clarity, distancing himself, another option came to mind, to drive away and keep on driving. That moment, Jim, in later years, identified as his crossroads. He should have driven away, letting Beth go, but wondered why he did not. He scarcely knew himself what drove him so relentlessly that evening.

His other teammates gathered at Klucky's to celebrate the end of football season. He lied to his parents, saying he planned to go, too. He lied to his teammates, telling them he needed to stay home and study for a test. No longer wanting to chase after

Beth and Tucker, he humbly joined them standing outside by their cars. One called out to him and, unlucky for Jim, brought up the rest of the story he missed earlier that day in the locker room. Tucker bragged about taking Beth up to what they all called, "The Hill," everyone's nickname for Spring Hill. Laughter and crude jokes commenced, but Jim heard none of it. That was the point when he first knew, whatever lived in him, so dark and so powerful, would one day destroy him.

Caught up in jealousy once more, he impulsively fled to his car. "I will die angry," he muttered aloud in bitter self-recrimination. Car engine roaring, he tore across the gravel. Tires screeching on the pavement, he sent his car fishtailing off down the highway, heading back to a turnoff he passed by earlier and would one day wish he passed again.

When Jim reached The Hill, he tried to locate Tucker's car. People began yelling at him to turn out his headlights. So, he parked anywhere he could and sat by himself. Enraged, he again became fed up with the whole thing, regretting ever meeting Beth.

Two boys came staggering by, saying, "Hey, look at the dope by himself! Wonder what he's planning on doing?!" They roared hysterically, obviously drunk, pointing at Jim, who was beyond humiliation.

He quickly looked around and got out of his car, not about to let Tucker try anything with Beth. He was going to find them, get Beth, and take her home. He endured more heckling, peering nonchalantly into each car he walked past. Some were too steamed up to see anything. Finally, to his horror, he spotted the car. Parked further off by itself under the trees, it rocked side to side, and Jim knew in an instant what that meant.

Darkness overcame his already-sinking heart. Like a child bullied to the breaking point, he broke. Seeing only the door handle, he flung it open, grabbed Tucker by the shirttail, dragged him out of the car, head banging, arms flailing, and Beth screaming. She scrambled to cover herself with whatever was on hand, which happened to be Tucker's jacket. Beth told Jim later she thought a lunatic attacked them. Jim reached into the car for her, while Tucker pulled up his pants and zipped them. Beth screamed again. Tucker grabbed hold of Jim and yanked him back out of the car. He punched him in the face, knocking him to the ground.

"What the hell are you doing?!" Tucker yelled at him in disbelief.

Jim lay there in the grass, moaning, hand to his face, watching dazed and helpless as Tucker turned to help Beth hastily gather up her clothes. He told her to hurry so they could drive away before Jim got up again. She slapped him in the face and pushed him away. Halfway dressed, she slipped on her shoes, grabbed up the rest of her clothes and purse. With Tucker's jacket held to cover her bare breasts, she stormed away as fast as she could walk. Jim struggled to get up and go after her.

Fights were common there, but their commotion had drawn attention from the other cars.

"Keep it down, why don't-cha?!"

"Hey! Take it somewhere else!"

Wolf calls and crude comments were directed at Beth. Tucker followed after her, begging and apologizing. With his head pounding, blood dripping down the side of his face, Jim managed to run up to them. He shoved Tucker aside in a final gesture, claiming the girl whom he had denied long enough and of whom he had been ashamed. He made his choice and, his father's death, over which he sorely ruminated, sadly sealed his fate.

Those days were long gone, but they marked the beginning of nearly fifteen years of frequent drunkenness. Jim hated no one now but himself. Very carefully he set Sylvia's shoes aside and, like a shot, fired his glass at the wall. Next, he picked up the bottle, drained it down his throat, and slammed it straight at the front window, glass crashing out onto the porch in a shattering, splintering explosion. This display signaled the beginning. He got up and knocked over furniture, pushed aside and smashed whatever he could. Nothing but junk in his careless rage, he hated it. Every scratched and stained and torn piece reminded him what a worthless bum he turned out to be. Everything he owned became unrecognizable through his uncontrolled fury. The blankets, he pulled off the bed, lifting the mattress off with them. Staggering, he reeled from drunken exhaustion. Tripping over the bed, he fell against it, collapsing into a heap onto the pile of faded and threadbare old bedding, instantly unconscious.

When he awoke, still drunk, his house sweltered in the stifling heat of the day. The chirping songs of birds wound their way down into the deepest shade of the trees. He dripped with sweat, his clothes soaked, so he dragged himself up off the floor and filled the bathtub full of cold water. In it he stepped and laid down, clothes and all. Slipping into unconsciousness again, he slowly sank lower and lower, until his head was completely under the water. No last thoughts were known to him. He merely fell away.

•　　•　　•

Leaving his body behind to grow cold and stiff, Jim stepped out of the water, not terrified, but confident and purposeful, at peace for the first time in years. Calling his dog, he walked away from his house never to return. Up the long driveway and onto the road beneath the towering elms, he led Shep, who always trusted him. Stopping at the porch of Sylvia's house he directed the German Shepherd, kindly talking to the dog as he knelt before him. Shep's head tipped to the left then to the right. He saw his master's vaguely luminous form, listening to him. Jim instructed him to wait for Sylvia. She would take care of him. Shep laid down and rested his head on his front paws, sighing with a whine.

"Goodbye, Shep. You be a good boy, you hear?"

Jim knew he was dead, no longer walking the earth as a man not really living. He understood what he needed to do. He accepted this transformation into the person, the man he always wished in life he could be. Fading into the rays of the sun streaming down as wide, golden beams of light amongst the trees, Jim Hart was more alive than he had ever been.

CHAPTER TWELVE

Tucker looked at his watch, wondering when Forty planned to get out of bed. He stood in his neglected garden holding a glass of ice water. Once more, he reviewed the unaddressed items on his checklist. Drawing the pencil out from behind his ear, he crossed out "dump" and "thrift store." He agreed with Forty, who saw the list and plainly stated, "That's too much to do, Tucker."

The sun climbed above the treetops, shining directly on him, it seemed, heating the air dramatically. He lamented the state of his garden and the precious shade receding into the thickets. Weeds knew nothing of time or the weatherman's predictions for record temperatures, he observed. Not the dandelions or the clover. His efforts to control them were frustrated by the looming heat of the day. They thrived in the humid air, growing stronger and more vigorous before his eyes, blooming and spreading their fine seeds efficiently and persistently. The grass in thick, green bunches went to seed behind his back. The brambles of blackberry vines and poison oak sprouted new tendrils from cut stems along the edge of his yard. At least, he reminded himself, he took care of the house first. Forty helped move furniture and hang pictures on the freshly painted walls, so there was little reason to complain. Nevertheless, the three, short days left in his vacation, slipped away into non-existence.

After encountering Jim and Beth's marriage and Forty and Sylvia's marriage, Tucker resigned himself to a life of bachelorhood. Dating fell to the bottom of his to-do list. He decided not to marry. Finishing the last of his water, he told himself, "Living alone's not so bad," and set his glass on the porch railing. Meant to console him, his words instead rang false and, therefore, threatened his hard-won, peaceful state of mind.

Perhaps, he thought, bending once more over the unwelcome crop of weeds, he was unhappy for reasons other than not having married. He pulled and he tugged and he ripped, piling the weeds wherever he tossed them, not paying any attention to his actions, only to his story mysteriously formulating anew.

The earth's fertile, loamy texture readily yielded roots. Where it lay packed like clay, long taproots broke. He twisted and wrenched them from the ground. He continued to try and understand his unhappiness, connected to something so clearly vague and yet so blindly obvious! He felt lonely much of the time, yet Forty's presence annoyed him. Clearly, he needed female companionship, bringing him back to where he started. The way to self-understanding, which he read in a book, required a different approach. Distrusting his heart and what it drove him to do, presented a problem. With sweat running down the sides of his face, he acknowledged this truth, "All in its time."

He did have a newfound appreciation for the people he knew, though their crumbling marriages prevented him from making any effort toward showing appreciation. His distancing from them was not out of fear or laziness, but a sense of what felt right and what presented itself at the time. Holding Sylvia in his arms, seemed to be the right thing to do. Further contemplation on the matter made him squirm. Helping Forty, the way it presented itself, turned out to be the right thing to do, he thought, though he was unclear whether it meant they were friends again. Thinking of Beth and Jim, he grimaced.

He stood up, stretched his back and straightened his knees, looking at the sun slowly rising higher above the elms lining the road across from his house. It was his way to track its movement, the sun, in its trek across the sky. Like the Greek and Roman myths he read in school, the sun brought each day a message, delivered across the sky in a chariot of gold. Horns blared and announced the message of the day, heralding the truth for all to heed. Or, maybe it was the bible, he briefly tried to recall. Never mind, he thought. This day, as the sun moved across the sky, a profound sense of purpose filled his awareness. He could not see all the events unfolding in the lives of those he knew and loved, but he could sense something greater than what lay within his view, slowly and magnificently coming to light. Like a great myth, he began to realize, and he grinned wide, shaking his head in amazement that no man could write a better story than the Lord, Himself. After all, his was truly a faith-inspired view of the world. He believed that Truth, written across the great dome of blue above, came from God.

"Tucker?"

Forty's voice again bore a childish quality. Though, when Tucker turned around, still grinning and enjoying everything the day miraculously brought forth, he nearly fell back, shocked by Forty's appearance. He looked extremely depressed.

"What is it, Forty?"

"I'm gonna go home now. Freckles needs to be at her own house."

"Well, all right. Do you need anything? Want some breakfast, er, lunch, before you go?"

"No."

With belongings in a paper sack carried in hand, Forty held Freckles close in his arms like a baby. He placed his feet carefully down each step, across Tucker's yard, before walking on the dirt road toward his home. With eyebrows drawn down in wonder, Tucker was baffled yet again. Fortuitous, his childhood friend, finally decided on his own to go home. He dimly wondered if Forty would be all right.

He resumed his task. Another hour or more of weed-pulling and Tucker succeeded at completely clearing his garden area. Despite the heat and humidity of the day, similar to the stifling, languid stillness of summer, he needed to dump the weeds somewhere. Wheelbarrow trips were made, pushing himself to finish this part of the job. Pausing to rest and wipe his brow, he smiled, affirming aloud, "We're in each other's lives again." Connection, give and take, commitment, and responsibility to his friends returned. Having retrieved these missing ingredients in his lonely, unhappy life, strengthened hope and inspired him.

This realization brought to mind those moments when something new is learned, like—he thrilled at this analogy, because it reminded him of something he forgot, something he found humorous, but life-changing. His first lesson on how babies are made, brought both connection and a sense of responsibility.

His father's words came to mind, giving him this important lesson, "It takes a man and a woman to make a child, son. You're a man now."

Tucker stood beside his bed, holding his hands away from him, covered in something that exploded out of him beneath the covers. He yelled in horror. His father rushed into his room, wanting to know what was the matter, then saw Tucker's hands. He merely said, while patting the air, "Now, now, Tucker," telling him to calm down. It was the dream he had, about a calendar hanging up at the filling station. He stared at the picture until the mechanic sauntered over, looked around, tore the picture off, folded it with his greasy, oily hands, and stuffed it in Tucker's shirt pocket.

"Happy birthday, kid," patting him on the head. It was not Tucker's birthday.

His father's lesson continued in grave seriousness, adding, "And, I expect Sylvia has become a woman by now."

He ceremoniously led Tucker to the bathroom, tossed a washcloth and towel over his son's shoulder, plugged the drain and started the bath water, closing the door as he walked out, saying, "We'll talk more about this later." Although, later never arrived.

Continuing to stay busy at work in his garden, loading a wheelbarrow with armloads of weeds and dumping out the contents, Tucker laughed aloud at the whole branch of memories that grew from that first, life-changing experience. The library always yielded answers. Off to the library, he searched for anything written on this serious business of how babies are made. What kind of book was he supposed to look for at the library? He wondered. What subject could he research? How could he know? He spent most of his life as a kid and only recently became a man. Giving up, he ended up leaving without any of his burning questions answered. Talking about it at school was unthinkable, he knew that much, but he had to find out more.

In the meantime, this unexplained mystery consumed his every thought. He wondered why his father brought Sylvia's name into this crucial matter. His mother was dead, but his sisters, Marjorie and Lois, were in high school. Marjorie, due to graduate, rarely made an appearance. Howard and Dewey were grown men, Howard married and living elsewhere. His last resort, his sister, Lois, called him, with an air of superiority, "Bug Face."

In his room he practically had all to himself, since Dewey occupied himself elsewhere, he spent a lot of time looking at the picture from the calendar. He learned through trial and error, to look at it when he was awake to avoid dreaming about it when he was asleep. Even so, over the school year, he became increasingly fascinated and curious about Sylvia. She entered his dreams. Reaching such a desperate stage in life required someone's aid. Needing to know more about girls, he decided to ask his sister.

"Lois?"

He tried to be serious and mature, hopefully impressing her with the gravity of the situation.

"What is it, *Bug* Face?"

She never took him seriously. Though her feminine side rarely showed itself, she sat there on her bed, admiring her latest hairstyle with a handheld mirror.

"I need to ask you something." He was resolute, not about to give up, because she was uninterested in listening to him. "It's about girls."

The mirror was flung out onto the bed beside her and Tucker thought either she was going to laugh or scream. She held her breath, contorting her face in such a strange manner, he wondered if she might be getting sick. She managed to contain what Tucker, as an adult, recognized as her hysterical glee.

"What do you want to know?"

"It's about Sylvia."

Lois listened carefully as Tucker began, "Dad said a man and a woman are needed to make a baby. He said, he expects Sylvia is a woman by now, but how can you tell? She looks like a regular kid to me. How can *she* make a baby?"

Now Lois was getting sick. Her face scrunched up in a frown as she looked here then there, avoiding looking directly at him. He stood his ground, waiting patiently for an answer.

Finally, and this was all she ever said to him ever again on the subject, yet it somehow changed forever how he looked at girls and women ever since, "Sylvia's not old enough. Besides, becoming a woman means a whole lot more than being able to bear children." She went back to her mirror.

Tucker got all the information from his sister he was going to get, so he turned to walk out of the room.

More to herself, Lois added an aside, while gazing in the mirror, "Give her a few years. You'll see for yourself whether or not she's a woman."

Back to the present, Tucker decided he did enough gardening for the day. Parking the wheelbarrow off to the side and placing the tools inside of it, he dared a glance toward Sylvia's house. In that moment, his checklist no longer mattered. Whatever he planned to do in the last days of his vacation receded into the background. He chose to recall how he felt when he held Sylvia close to him, his head touching her's. He remembered the first time he kissed her, and the second time and, most definitely, the third and last time. Quite unexpectedly, he, all of a sudden knew in his heart that he loved her. He always loved her.

After washing up a bit, he checked his watch. He thought he would be neighborly and see if Forty was doing all right, though he instantly caught that excuse. He wanted to see Sylvia again, now that he knew the truth. He willingly remained innocent of any underlying motives.

CHAPTER THIRTEEN

Shep ran out of Forty and Sylvia's house, barking loudly, before running back into the house, still barking. Soon, Freckles came stumbling out, with Forty close behind. The sight of Jim Hart's dog, put Tucker on edge, thinking he might be in the house.

"Isn't that Jim's dog?"

"Tucker! Tucker!"

Forty ignored the question, hobbling toward him in bare feet that felt every pebble and stone. He told Tucker what he discovered.

"Shep is here and my wife is gone! She took her suitcase and- and some clothes!" He broke down into incoherent mumblings, behaving almost delirious. Tucker grabbed a vial of prescription medicine out of Forty's hand, which he thought he hid, and read the label. It was something for pain, though not the same as what he confiscated earlier.

"Something's wrong, Tucker! What am I gonna do?! What happened to my wife?!"

"Forty! Calm down!"

Tucker helped Forty inside and over to the sofa. He reassured him. "Don't worry. We'll find out what happened. Okay?"

Freckles left piles and puddles across the wood flooring. First, she chewed on a stick. She lost interest in that, plopping herself down beside the sofa, gnawing aggressively on its bottom edge. The bag of dog food lay knocked over in the kitchen, its contents spilling onto the floor. Shep and Freckles trotted in behind Tucker and began to eat from the pile. An industrious procession of ants trailed to and from the kibble. Tucker closed his eyes and sighed deeply. Thinking what to do, he picked up the bag and rolled it closed, set it on the washing machine out back, swept up the kitchen floor, cleaned up the dog's messes, and gathered up whatever Freckles dragged inside.

In the kitchen, he called the sheriff, keeping his voice low. He automatically assumed Jim and Sylvia ran off together, alluding to the possibility over the phone, but kept the assumption to himself, for now. He wanted the sheriff present, before he mentioned it to Forty. He also needed some helpful advice concerning his friend's state of mind. He worried Forty might hurt himself. For that reason, he kept the pills, though guessing Forty probably hid another vial somewhere.

Remembering his brother's suicide attempts after Dewey returned from the war, he recognized in Forty those same overwhelming, emotional waves of grief and despair his brother exhibited. His brother told the priest who visited him, "I'm drownin', Father. I'm sinkin' and I can't make it stop." Dewey succeeded at killing himself in 1953. Tucker did not want to lose another soul to such a terrible tragedy.

Pacing the living room floor on a hot day, he watched over Forty. His friend sat staring out the front window, mumbling, dropping his head down low, mumbling some more. Tucker found himself unable to manage Forty's woeful disposition, except to suggest he get some rest, promising to bring Sylvia home. The pills Forty took put him to sleep. Tucker sat on the floor, leaning back against the bed, looking out the window.

The heat of the day increased until it felt unbearable. The sun beat down upon the front of the old house, baking its walls. Shep panted loudly, nervous and skittish, on constant alert, ears turning this way and that. Freckles lay in Tucker's lap, looking generally bored or worried. He was undecided as to which.

Nearly an hour after he called the sheriff, a car pulled up outside. Car doors opened and slammed shut. Shep bolted in a frantic scratch across the wood floor, running out of the room and down the stairs, barking. His loud assault on the newcomers startled Freckles, so she started shaking. Tucker set her aside. He quickly drew his watch out of his pocket, noted the time, and went out to greet the sheriff. Bumbling and rolling along like a fat, tumbling ball of fur, Freckles nearly fell down the stairs.

Outside, two deputies leaned back against their car. Shep continued barking, so they respectfully kept their distance. Tucker approached the dog to quiet him. Once he took hold of its collar, Shep wheeled around and nipped him on the hand, then ran back into the house. Tucker stood there in stinging pain, eyes squeezed shut, while holding his maimed hand, he imagined, though the skin was only red. Freckles let out a puppyish yap. A fly distracted her, so she hopped away to chase after it. The deputies tried coaxing the yapping puppy to come up to them. She backed away until she bumped her rear into the bottom porch step, scaring herself, then spun around to run back into the house with her tail between her legs.

Tucker practically collapsed onto the porch, his own head hanging low. Two mild-mannered officers were not exactly the cavalry he imagined showing up to save the day, but there was no time to wait around for them to prove their worth, Tucker believed. Something needed to be done and it needed to be done now.

Bob, the senior deputy, spoke up first, hands on his bony hips. "Well, Jim, what's all this about Forty's wife and Jim Hart?"

His serious tone made a much better impression, so, heaving a deep sigh and reminding Bob to call him, "Tucker," he began telling them all he knew. He was sure to stress not to tell Forty what his wife had been up to with Jim Hart.

The deputy had an investigative approach. "Did you see them together?"

The question annoyed Tucker. He never saw Sylvia and Jim together. But, he wanted to be cooperative, hoping to help them look for Sylvia. So, he reluctantly answered, "No."

"Have you ever seen them together?"

"No."

"Well, how do you know they were foolin' around?"

Tucker became uneasy, because this involved his own unscrupulous actions and, although nervous about bringing the subject out into the open, he answered, "Because, I've seen things." The deputy's eyebrows raised. Embarrassed, Tucker rephrased what he said. "I've *witnessed*," he thought official-sounding words might prove more credible, "Sylvia behaving," and he had to be careful what he said, "in a secretive manner."

Bob glanced over at the other deputy walking about the yard instead of paying attention. He called out to him, snapping his fingers, "Hey, Stoney!"

Stoney was a new deputy, "fresh out of diapers," Bob complained to his superiors, mad at them for giving him a baby-faced rookie. Speculating over the origin of the name, "Stoney," he decided not to ask. Stoney rejoined them and Bob continued, "Now, Tucker, I think we're gonna have to go over this one more time." He added, "Damn, it's hot today! Why don't we go talk in the shade," pointing to the yard on the side of the house.

They moved the fledgling investigation over to a set of broken-down outdoor furniture clustered beneath the deep shade of the woodland's edge. Stoney sat on the rickety picnic table with his feet propped on a broken bench seat.

Bob reiterated the facts, "Now, I'm well aware Forty's wife is not the purest woman on the block, but we have to stick to what you've actually witnessed."

Trying to contain his emotions, Tucker shared his observations made over the years, including Sylvia's pattern of going by the newspaper office, sometimes heading down the path toward Jim's house. He restrained himself from sharing the look Sylvia gave Jim in church last Easter. What he did share was true. Relieved of his burden, he relaxed. The deputies listened intently, with Bob asking questions along the way and having Tucker tell him more regarding Forty's behavior, which Tucker did. Finally acknowledging the truth, Tucker trusted the two officers knew what to do despite the impression they made upon their arrival.

They returned to the front yard. Bob grabbed his radio to call in a request for someone to help with Forty. He did not report Sylvia's disappearance.

Tucker advanced aggressively toward Bob, instantly angry, "What about Sylvia?!" He demanded that Bob go look for her.

"Now, now, Tucker. We have to get to the bottom of this first. We can't just drive off chasing after people. We don't know if there's been any foul play. That hasn't exactly been established."

He reminded Tucker of his father, saying, "Now, now, son. Calm down. Everything's going to be all right."

He pleaded with the deputy, keeping his voice low, "I've had about all I can handle." He threw his hands up in the air, giving up, "I-I don't know," and let them drop to his sides. He looked away, then directly into the deputy's eyes, without fear, as though trying to make sure Bob understood him, "I couldn't bear it if something happened to her."

Bob looked shocked, eyes widened and eyebrows raised, hearing what sounded to him like an affirmation of love for a woman who was not his wife, but of the man who lay in bed, distraught from grief! He pointed out something to Tucker, who neglected to take it into consideration before he said to the deputy what he had.

"Do you realize what you're saying, young man?" Bob was more than twenty years older than Tucker. Tucker looked puzzled, so Bob made it clear, "From what you've told me, some might conclude, not only are you in love with another man's wife, but your own behavior paints a rather sordid picture." He paused to gauge Tucker's reaction, then continued, "I do believe, if you were giving your testimony in a court of law, telling about all the *spying* you've been doing, behind *this man's back,*" pointing toward the house, "you'd not only paint yourself as a suspect, but as someone who is downright *guilty!*"

Tucker jumped to defend himself, shouting, "Now, wait a minute! I haven't done anything wrong! I didn't do anything with her and it wasn't me she ran off with!"

Bob argued the point further, "You're beginning to sound like a jealous man, Tucker! A jealous man who—who feels *cheated!*"

Tucker reeled with a fury he had no idea was inside of him until that moment. His hands were balled into fists, of which he was unaware. He walked around a bit to calm himself, rub his face that somehow had not been shaved in days, while Bob talked low with the other deputy.

Earlier in the day he finally admitted to himself he loved Sylvia. Now, the deputy accused him of wrongdoing! He shook his head in disbelief how this turned into something far different than what he imagined that morning, that they were friends again. Discouraged, and berating himself for acting hopelessly naïve, he turned cynical, knowing Forty's current behavior would pass and his belligerence toward Tucker speedily resume. Sylvia, well, she would continue to ignore him, like she always had.

He recalled an incident that took place in high school in his junior year. Jim discovered how Tucker felt about Sylvia, feelings that were more than those for a friend. Jim started up in the locker room, commenting on how pretty Sylvia was getting to be and "too bad her aunt hates you, Stewart," laughing derisively, "and your dad, too, for that matter!" Not stopping there, he proceeded to sink even lower. "Now, as for me, I can pretty much come and go as I please, where Sylvia's concerned and, lately, I've been *very* pleased." Then, came the cruel jab, "Might as well face it. You'll never be good enough for her," and he strutted confidently out of the locker room, turning at the doorway to get one last look at Tucker's face. Tucker refused to give him the satisfaction of meeting Jim's eyes with his own, but inside he hurt to the core.

It hurt, because Tucker believed what Jim said. No one needed to tell him that Sylvia's aunt despised him and his father. Judging by the way Sylvia avoided him, maybe she thought the same. After their chance encounter in the woods one autumn day in high school, Sylvia stayed away from him more than ever, even shunned him. Rumors spread around school, going on about all the boys with whom she shamelessly associated. Tucker refused to believe it, but saw it for himself on more than one occasion.

He said to himself, "Well, I guess I didn't know her as well as I thought." This moment of humility was swept aside, as he wallowed in self-pity. "It's true. I wasn't *good enough* for her," referring to his performance as a lover and his never having lived up to his name, something he always believed his mother expected of him. In truth, she never thought of her sons in that manner. Tucker knew that. His mother never expected him to be adored by all the girls like some kind of movie star. She wanted him, and all her sons, to grow up to be good men others would respect, who would fight to uphold the truth, no matter what the cost. Wondering if he was living up to his name—

Bob interrupted his thoughts, quietly advising Tucker, "You ought to think about what I said." Tucker humbly nodded in agreement and the deputy went on, "A nurse is coming over to take care of Forty, so that should alleviate some of the burden you've been carrying lately." He stopped and waited to make sure Tucker was listening. "Me and Stoney, here, are gonna go over to, uhh, Hart's place, see what we can find out. His dog probably just got off his chain. I doubt there's anything more to it than that." Tucker weakly agreed with him. Bob thought he looked pretty pathetic, shook his head, and snapped his fingers at Stoney, signaling him it was time to go and he better hurry.

They drove on toward the Hart's house. Soon afterward, a nurse in a white uniform arrived to help with Forty. She brought a medical bag and a small suitcase. She was the same nurse with whom Beth had gone to stay. She felt sorry for Forty, treated him once before. When she heard they were looking for a nurse to do some short-term home care for Fortuitous Sumner, she inquired further and readily volunteered. No one objected. The nursing staff heard from Beth more than they cared to know. Before the nurse left, the head nurse advised not to get involved in their private affairs, only to do her job. She tried not to show how pleased she was to be able to see Fortuitous again.

Once she arrived, seeing Tucker gave her a start. She admired his physique, while they casually talked about Tucker's father. He led her up to Forty's room, commenting on the fact that neither of the dogs were barking. She didn't hear a word he said, still lost in her dreams about Tucker Stewart, the man she openly admired and secretly adored.

CHAPTER FOURTEEN

Jim Hart's dilapidated old house greeted the two deputies. A broken front window, glass riddling the porch, and a busted whiskey bottle in its midst, provided a warning. Stalling, Bob turned off the car, pulled out his handkerchief to wipe the sweat from his forehead and neck, and sighed.

In all his years as a deputy, nowhere did he see a town so plagued with problems. Mostly alcoholism and adultery, which seemed to run in families, he observed. He reported few wife-beating cases, or children getting hurt by their drunken, unfaithful parents. Drug problems sweeping the nation's college towns and urban centers missed the sleepy, yet very "quirky, little town," he said. When offered jobs in other counties, he always declined. He liked Edenville, and he liked the people, too.

Bolstering his courage, he led the way, saying, "Let's go and see what happened here."

The house looked abandoned, so Bob grew wary and concerned once he shut the door to the patrol car. Shep made a sudden appearance, running up to the house.

"What the—!" Shocked, Bob looked at the other deputy, asking, "Can you believe all this?"

Shep furiously dug at the bottom of the screen door in a state of panic, whining and barking, frantically banging against it, trying to get into the house. He sat and barked into the air and at Bob.

Stepping close to the door, glimpsing the wreckage inside, Bob instantly drew back.

"Oh, boy."

He put his hand to the other deputy's arm, telling him to wait. Retreating step by step off the porch, he took some time to recover from the shock of seeing the unexpected horror. Hands on his hips, he gazed toward the forest leading up into the mountains. Something about the trees always brought calm. Behind him, Shep paced and whined.

Offhandedly, Bob said, "You know, my wife's been wanting to go see that big lake everybody talks about. Maybe I'll take her this weekend. That'd be nice."

Squinting from the bright sun in his eyes, Bob turned to look up at Stoney, where he stood on the porch, and tried to smile. Stoney frowned in response, slowly lowering his gaze, only to encounter the glass strewn across the porch.

Giving up, Bob gave a jerk of his head, saying, "Okay. Let's try this again."

Shep went straight to the bathroom doorway, barking and whining at the deputies to get their attention. They picked their way around piles of smashed debris, glass crunching underfoot. Careful where they placed their feet, they gradually advanced further into the house. They looked around the living room, seeing the bedding strewn across the back of the house. Swatting at flies, Bob quickly checked in the bathroom, got one look at a body in the bathtub full of water, grabbed the other deputy's arm and pulled him back toward the front door.

"Come on. We need to call this one in."

Stoney followed hurriedly behind him, then ran off behind the car. Bob, in a daze, blankly stared in that direction. Under his breath, he asked himself, "What am I gonna do?"

The two deputies stood in place, absently watching Shep run off up the driveway. Shaking himself out of his daze, Bob radioed, rather soberly, into the sheriff's substation to report on what they found. He told them where Jim's wife worked. She needed to be notified. The coroner's office at the main sheriff's station was over by the county hospital, so the deputy knew they were in for a long wait.

The only thought Bob dared to venture, he voiced aloud to his partner, "Well, Stoney, look's like we're gonna miss lunch."

During their long wait, the substation called to say the rest home informed them Beth quit her job, apparently after leaving her husband for cheating on her. He requested they send someone out to find her. His voice quieted when he said, "We gotta let her know what happened," stressing they make sure to question her. First Tucker, now Beth, he groaned.

Bob wanted more than anything to leave this tragic scene. He saw death before, car accidents, mostly, but nothing in his entire life prepared him for what he saw in that house. He struggled to get over the shock, though he would never, ever forget that scene.

Quietly and uneventfully, the coroner's team finally arrived. Later, a homicide detective with his assistant, followed by another patrol car with two more deputies approached those assembling around the cars. Their gradual approach, driving toward the house, sadly resembled a funeral procession. It gave Bob a jolt.

Deputy Sheriff Bob Carson only ever wanted in life to be an officer of the law, and have no more difficulty at that than driving around the countryside, taking liquor away from minors. What he knew, unfortunately, would place Tucker, Beth, and Sylvia in handcuffs. Tucker bore no more guilt than falling in love with a woman nearly every—well, as for Beth, he dismissed her easily. She finally left her husband, as had Sylvia, he imagined, something they both should have done years ago.

Doing some quick figuring, based on what he uncovered, the deputy planned to leave Tucker out of it completely. He told his partner to go wait in the car. Seeing the detective looking their way, he vaguely added, "We'll be leaving soon. They won't need us anymore." In truth, he wanted the inexperienced officer kept out of the discussion.

Walking toward one another, the detective drew out a notepad and pen, stopped and waited for the deputy's report. With his back to the patrol car, Bob began by telling the detective the victim's name.

"That's Jim Hart. He was married, uhh, to Beth Hart. Used to work over at the rest home as a cook, until recently."

The detective nodded, familiar with the place, and urged him to go on, jotting down information as he listened.

"They both had quite a drinking habit. We've been on several calls involving locals drinking and fighting. Hart's usually in the middle of it." This is where things got tricky. He offhandedly added, hoping the detective would not make something of it, "Apparently, she left him recently." Despite the deputy's attempts at behaving nonchalant, the detective instantly perked up.

"When?"

"I don't know. Another man called, claiming his wife was missing, named Sylvia Sumner. According to him, she took a suitcase, some clothing and personal items, and left somewhere."

The detective caught what the deputy was getting himself into, "What does she have to do with any of this?"

"Well . . ." The deputy merely acted as though he was getting around to explaining and the detective interrupted. He continued, saying, "Hart's dog showed up at their house. Her husband, Forty Sumner, was all worked up. He said she left without a word." Finding it too difficult to avoid mentioning Tucker, he merely concluded, "Apparently, they were having some problems," and left it at that. He realized his attempt to avoid bringing them into the story, only made him feel guilty, dragging their names in anyway.

"Okay, so let me get this straight." The detective went over what he understood had happened, "You got a call today about a woman believed to be missing. Hart's dog had shown up at their house—when did you say?"

"I-I don't know when, but me and my partner drove over here to find out why." The deputy thought he was already losing the battle to protect Tucker, a man he would have called his friend, in all probability, if he lived in Edenville.

"All right." The detective proceeded to finish repeating to the deputy what he heard, as Jim's wrapped-up body was carried outside and placed in the back of a truck. He was asked something by his assistant, turned to answer him, then went back to talking with the deputy. "So, a guy reports his wife is missing, Hart's dog showed up at their house, and you came down here to investigate, and found all of this," motioning to the body and the house, "right?"

"Yes, that's correct." The deputy, relieved, thought it made sense without involving Tucker Stewart.

Even so, the detective's job required him to get to the bottom of the story. After checking on what they found, talking with the coroner, he let the deputy know what else needed to be done.

"Well, Bob, from how things look in there, the coroner agrees it was probably a suicide. But, until we talk to his wife and—who'd you say he was? Fort—"

Bob readily answered, "Fortuitous Sumner. But he's not going to be of any help."

"Oh?" No one decided for the detective what was or wasn't important. "Why's that?"

"Well, he's—he's unwell. The man's—" Bob wanted the detective to leave the poor man in peace. "We've got a nurse taking care of him and he might be sleeping, or something."

Interrupting Bob, the detective said, "Well, why don't you lead the way over there and we'll see what's what." Anxious to continue his investigation, he added, "Then, I'd like to head up to the rest home and find out more about this poor guy's wife."

Getting into the patrol car and driving away, Bob hoped Beth and Sylvia left town long ago and Tucker stayed home. To play it safe, he instructed the junior deputy, "Lot of excitement your first day, Stoney. Better just watch and listen. Okay?" Stoney merely nodded his head and said, "Yes, sir."

The other deputies were left behind to guard the house. The truck left earlier, rolling away behind the county coroner on their way to the morgue.

Jim Hart's final hours concluded under the scrutiny of a medical examiner. His last day ended on a stainless steel table, stripped of all the material trappings of the world. Now a victim listed in an official report, he lay no longer a man, but a corpse, no longer holding within whatever made it alive more than a beating heart could instill.

That essence of who he was, whom Sylvia never saw, Tucker Stewart would later strive to understand and one day come to know. First, he needed to face the man he always took to be his rival, but with whom he fought against more like a brother. The opportunity now presented itself for Tucker to learn that Jim Hart might very well have been his best friend.

CHAPTER FIFTEEN

Freckles tried to follow Shep running down the road behind the patrol car. After a couple hundred feet, she stopped, twirling around to see what happened to Shep, but he was nowhere to be seen. She plunked down on her rear in the middle of the road and began to whine. She scratched behind her ear. A woolly caterpillar, crawling its many-footed way across the road, attracted her and she followed it. This is how Tucker spotted her, hopping playfully a ways down the road. He walked over to her, picked her up, wondering if Shep had gone home.

At Forty's house, the nurse assured him she would be fine without his help. He fixed sandwiches, volunteered to take Forty's puppy home with him, and left. No sooner did he walk away, before Shep came running up, panting hard and looking increasingly agitated and worn out.

"Where've you been?"

Now, Tucker had two dogs to watch. A greater concern, he quickly figured the heat of the day reached its peak an hour ago. The dust along the road hung in the air and sweat ran down the sides of his face, forming muddy rivulets, coursing through the dirt coating his skin. Fortunately, he thought, the sun made its downward trek across the sky, sinking behind the trees. Once his home came into view, he gladdened at the sight, seeing it settled comfortably within the shade.

Since the dogs were both accustomed to having full run indoors, bringing Freckles in and leaving Shep outside, proved impossible. Once he tried it, Shep began scratching, digging, and even gouging at the bottom of his front door.

"All right! All right! Come on in."

Shep tiredly sauntered into Tucker's once-private abode. Giving in, he welcomed them both with a bowl of water and an old blanket dropped onto the kitchen floor. Thankfully, though he knew they were both exhausted from running who-knows-where-and-back, they slept soundly after the commotion that had taken place.

Grateful for a reprieve—he never had a dog in his whole life, let alone a puppy to raise, he also needed to take a nap. The heat within the closed-up house was unbearably oppressive. He could hardly breathe. He opened windows in every room and, when he opened the front windows, he saw the coroner's car and a truck drive past. The time read between two and three o'clock. Out of curiosity, he went outside to look. He wanted to find out what happened, but the dogs were sleeping. Reminding himself they needed the rest, he let it go. Stuck at his house, babysitting other people's dogs, he waited for them to wake up on their own. It never occurred to him the coroner's presence was connected to Shep being on the loose.

He took care of some of his chores, made up a grocery list, then did something he thought may not be his place. Curious what Forty's boss thought of his absence from work, he telephoned the factory. Tucker thought it might be helpful to look in on Forty's job, if he still had a job. Apparently, he learned from talking with a secretary, Sylvia took care of things months ago. Having never used his vacation time and having used very little of his sick days allowed, Forty accumulated a lot of paid time-off. Sylvia told them she needed his help taking care of her sick father who lived out of town. With this concern happily addressed and a nurse at his house, Tucker had no need to worry about Forty.

Reminded of Sylvia and her mysterious disappearance, he sat down at the kitchen table with a tall glass of ice cold water and revisited what the deputy said earlier. He sounded like a guilty man, cheated out of the one and only woman he ever loved. Tucker thought he must sound pretty pathetic and tried not to dwell on it. It surprised him, how angry he got when confronted about his feelings for Sylvia. He smiled and shook his head, because the more he tried to avoid the subject of Sylvia, the more she appeared in his thoughts.

Searching, instead, for other instances when he became angry, a pattern formed out of a string of memories, a theme explaining why he got so mad. His mother's illness before she died, he was never told. A co-worker at the newspaper quit, but no one informed him. The man was merely absent until Tucker learned the truth on his own and confronted the others in the office, only to be faced with their guilty silence. Being kept in the dark, kept from knowing, angered him. Secrecy angered him. He needed to be told the truth. He fought for it. His passion, in this light, defended the truth, rallying around a purpose, the gold he must forge in life, directed bit by bit into what was written across the dome of the world.

A message drifted upon the day's fading sunlight. Looking out the kitchen window upon the sunny fields beyond the alleyway, he came to know his purpose. Not in words, but a sense that, though he may not ever know of all its parts, through friendship, he would somehow play a part. This truth, he knew.

It struck him, Sylvia's disappearance might have something to do with her father, Robert Cadwallader. He thought the man might still be alive, because his own father spoke with him within the last four or five years. His father told him that Caddie stayed at the rest home for a time while he sobered up. According to his dad, that was not his first attempt. Before his father's condition worsened a few years ago, which resulted in his stay there, and when he easily communicated, he wanted to visit Sylvia's father. They told him Robert Cadwallader refused to allow anyone to see him. He disappeared and, no one, as far as Tucker knew, heard of him since.

The dogs slept for over an hour. Tucker continued carrying out minor chores around the house. He even got a bath and finally shaved. Why a coroner came to their end of town posed a mystery he wished to solve. He wanted to ask his neighbors if they knew anything. Although, to be alone in his peaceful, quiet home was too good to disturb. He completed his grocery list, wondering how to manage the dogs while he went to the store. Dog food was at the top of the list. Shep ate a lot. The bag at Forty's house was almost empty, since so much had to be swept up and discarded. Here, he only brought a small amount for Freckles to eat.

The Sumner's house on his mind again, he recalled noticing, while he made lunch, that their food was surprisingly fresh. This observation made an impression on him and how he viewed, not her habits, but Sylvia's character. He rolled his eyes, because it seemed the more he tried to forget about her, the more he tried to think about her! Too lulled by the heat and boredom, he decided not to worry about whether he was pathetic, obsessed, or in love, and let himself drift along in peaceful contemplation.

About Sylvia, here was this woman who, in his estimation, had impeccable taste in style and dress and, while excellent care was obviously given to all she did, they were only *certain* things. For instance, she obviously paid great attention to the ironing and the wash. The food, though dwindling in supply, was arranged neatly and well-organized in the cupboards and in the refrigerator. Walking around their house, in bleak contrast, inconsistencies leapt out in every room. These differences only made him want to know more about her, who the girl he once thought he knew had become.

While the house was fairly tidy, it was not nearly as clean as he kept his own house. Not one single photograph, painting, or any picture or wall hanging graced their home. Except for a mirror on the back of the bathroom door, the walls were bare. He discovered the boxes of Detective's Digest missing. Their absence disappointed him, because he needed something to read to wile away the time, while he waited for the deputies to arrive. Evidently, Forty and Sylvia did not care to read books, which Tucker preferred over comic books and magazines. Not one book existed in their strangely empty home. He kept telling himself not to be so much of a snoop and start looking in drawers and closets. In the kitchen, where his activities centered, other inconsistencies presented themselves. His cupboards were stocked with a basic array of pans, bowls, etc. Their's were practically bare, more like a kitchenette in a roadside motel.

He marveled at her efficiency, grateful for everything she did. Yet, to dismiss what stood out so blatantly, the unlived aspect of their existence, the space that overwhelmed what little filled their home, he deemed inconceivable. Something terribly wrong demanded attention . . . though he was not sure what. The feeling it gave Tucker, he tried to understand, reminded him of one time when he saw his father walking hurriedly over to Sylvia's, before her mother died.

Sylvia stopped by Forty's house on their way home from school, but Tucker's father always told him to come straight home. When he walked through the front door, he looked for his dad, but the house was quiet, no one home. Catching movement outside the kitchen window, he spotted his dad hurrying across the backyard over to Sylvia's house. Her father joined the service. In his absence, Tucker's dad helped Sylvia's mother. Apparently not very handy fixing things that kept getting broken, she called upon him frequently. This time, Tucker walked out the back door, innocent and only wanting to ask his father if he could get something to eat and join his friends at Forty's house. Onward to Sylvia's next door, onto their wash porch, as was his habit, and the funny feeling washed over him.

He heard Sylvia's mother laughing in a way he never heard her laugh. Well, his mother used to laugh that way when his father came up from behind and, squeezing her waist, began kissing her on the neck.

The door was ajar and, yet innocent of what was going on, he nevertheless felt compelled to be cautious, proceeding slowly, gently pushing the door open until he was in the kitchen. He heard his father's voice and that of Sylvia's mother, Charity. Sylvia's relatives were given funny names, like Uncle Prosperous, a name Tucker could never forget. Sylvia told him long ago, her grandpa named them all and, her mother, Charity, was named during a particularly penniless period in their lives.

What Tucker saw when he tiptoed across the kitchen, well aware his curiosity was turning him into a nosey spy, was his father and Sylvia's mother absolutely and irrefutably naked, without a stitch of clothing on, not socks, not shirts, nothing. He froze at the doorway to the bedroom where his father and Charity were passionately involved in doing "It." He knew, even at ten years old, what they were doing, the big "It," the word kids only whispered and always found so incredibly funny. Tucker was not laughing. He was crying and tore himself away to hurry outdoors, running across the street behind their house, toward the orchards, until he could run no more. He uncontrollably began rubbing dirt all over himself, weeds, grass, even rolling in the mud, anything to scrape off what he felt.

With grimy arms and face, and grass-stained clothes, he hid until dark in Fort Sumner, crying with his knees drawn up and his arms hiding his face buried in shame. Sylvia and Forty saw him crawl inside their hide-out, so they joined him, sitting in respectful silence beside their best friend. They had all done the same many times. Fort Sumner was their place to do what they wanted when they wanted and needed. It demanded an unspoken, unwritten law, a code of respect and honor. Though they had no idea as to the seriousness about which he was crying, they never asked, also part of the code, and he never told.

Now a grown man, he judged that Forty had plenty of serious matters to cry about as a child, and he definitely knew Sylvia had. Ashamed, sad, disappointed, it was difficult to label what he felt about Sylvia and Forty's home life, but he did not like the feeling any more now than when he was a boy. With a sinking feeling growing in his chest, he appreciated the distraction the dogs provided as they began to stir, get up, stretch and yawn, and immediately need to be let outside.

CHAPTER SIXTEEN

The nurse told the officers her patient should not be disturbed. Forty's afternoon nap, thankfully, thwarted the detective's persistent questioning. Pleased, Bob next led the way to Spring Hill Residence & Infirmary. Confident in Beth Hart's absence from the rest home, he and his junior deputy steadily rolled along in the sheriff's car, followed by the detective in an unmarked, black Oldsmobile. Dust raised in their wake, in spite of Bob's efforts to prevent it.

Eager to see the end of that long and weary day, Bob nearly relaxed until he spotted Tucker coming out of his house unexpectedly. He showed considerable interest in their presence, craning his neck and staring at them. Grumbling to himself, anxious to part company with the detective, making him sweat over what he knew and loathed mentioning, Bob dreaded interference from that "love-sick and obsessed Tucker Stewart."

The deputy proceeded onward. He purposely made no indication he knew Tucker or had any reason to know him. Merely a curious onlooker, Bob told himself, keeping his eyes directed straight ahead.

He casually commented to his partner, "That was some story he told, wasn't it? Sheesh!"

The junior deputy quietly chuckled in response and shook his head.

Thus reassured, what Tucker knew about the Hart's, Forty, and Sylvia, Bob mentally noted to disregard.

Once they arrived at the rest home, a call from the dispatcher came in over the radio. An incident down at Klucky's roadhouse required their attention, something about a man seen attempting to start a fire. Bob let out a loud sigh of relief.

In the meantime, Tucker called the dogs and closed up the house. Proceeding over to Forty's, thankful the road was now shaded, he brought back to mind seeing the coroner's car. Its presence meant someone died who lived on his street, which explained the deputy's baffling behavior. Bob was evidently called away by more important matters, he concluded. Speculating further, he figured Forty and Sylvia's domestic problems consequently lost Bob's attention.

Arriving at Forty's house, Tucker hesitated before entering, placing one foot on the threshold. After the long, hot day, the wood door frame yet felt warm to his touch where he grasped it lightly. A sense of wanting to completely let go, overcame him. It passed through his awareness, quickly forgotten, and he stepped inside the house.

Forty awoke from his nap, currently going up the stairs with Freckles, praising the puppy, his voice lowered. Tucker noticed he seemed a bit subdued. Lacking experience with those recovering from being under the influence of anything, except alcohol, his friend's withdrawn demeanor left him shaken. Pale and visibly depressed, Tucker assumed the signs pointed to Forty's continued reaction to his wife's infidelity.

Tucker struggled to contain his anger. He wondered why Sylvia's own husband was not mad. Seeing the nurse in the kitchen, getting herself some water, he crossed the living room to speak with her about Forty's behavior. She said, where addicts were concerned, "there's no such thing as being too sure." Why she referred to Fortuitous as an addict, challenged Tucker's opinion.

Shep continued to trail closely behind Tucker wherever he went. Close behind Shep, Freckles happily tagged along. Tucker collected the trash to put in the garbage cans behind the house. He washed the few dishes sitting by the sink, already attracting ants. He debated doing more than that. Forty's mood troubled him. When he returned downstairs, Tucker noticed an oppressive pall fell upon the whole room by the man's grim presence. The nurse talked privately with Forty in the living room, suggesting that, perhaps, a short stay at Spring Hill might help. Tucker reacted with disbelief, overhearing her likening a stay at an infirmary to a vacation. Even more surprising, Forty responded favorably to her suggestion.

Rushing to object, he hurried into the living room, saying, "What?!"

Ignoring Tucker, Forty went into the bathroom and closed the door. The nurse took Tucker aside, quietly informing him that Forty was at risk. At risk for what, Tucker wanted to know, so she explained. She said Forty would reach a point when he would do anything to get his hands on some more pain medication. She added, he needed to be under observation and Spring Hill would be the best place for him.

Exasperated, Tucker shook his head, still objecting to the idea. He thought the nurse was overly cautious and even downright melodramatic about the whole thing. Yet, he remembered the instances he caught Forty dumping pills into his hand in blind desperation.

"Well, if Forty wants to go there, I'll drive him, and take care of the dogs in his absence."

Coming out of the bathroom, Forty spoke morosely, "Shep ain't my dog. I don't want him around here anymore," and plopped himself onto the sofa, too over-wrought to care about anything or anybody. He slouched down low with his hand slightly covering his face, exhausted.

Tucker halfway expected Forty to add that Shep was a bad influence on Freckles, as he might have done in his previous, childlike way. He wondered where that went to, as he studied the Fortuitous Sumner who sat before him now.

Something caught his eye, a folded piece of paper or note on the floor, under the edge of the sofa. Forty stood up to get ready to leave, but quickly sat back down. Tucker noticed him, ever so slightly, pushing it further under the sofa with his foot. Unsure what to do, Tucker hastily decided he would check on it later. Meanwhile, he needed to keep an eye on Forty until they were driving away. He recalled this was the Forty he saw driving into town, leaving his car running, while he went into the drugstore, later having a vial of pills. Forty was hooked on those pills, Tucker realized. He humbly respected the nurse, who spoke from experience when she said he needed to be under the care of a doctor. What Tucker had yet to learn were all the reasons for Forty's moodiness. He would hear of them soon enough.

The nurse excused herself to go upstairs to pack her things. When she returned, she let Forty know what he needed to bring, so he went upstairs, shortly reappearing with a grocery sack in his grasp. Tucker resumed his chores, sticking to his original plan to purchase any needed items. Crossing the room, he caught Forty glaring at him. The unwelcomeness of his presence, as he pretended to feel useful, was made clear by that one glance. He crumpled up the list he had started to write, tossed it into the trash, and left the kitchen.

Encountering Forty's obvious anger toward him, Tucker asked, "Is anything wrong, Forty? I mean, did I do something wrong?"

Forty's jaw dropped, looking at him with the strangest expression. It reminded him of a television show he once saw, in which the sergeant of the platoon gave one of his men the same look and yelled, "What do you think I am?! Stupid?!" Like a split-second punch in the chest, it caught Tucker off guard and left him stunned.

Forty went outside. The nurse was already there waiting by the car. Any thoughts Tucker had about helping around the house or with the dogs, like he suspected would happen, fizzled into the old pattern he used to know only a few months ago. Their temporary relationship was not a renewal of anything, except Tucker's commitment to Sylvia, his sense of responsibility toward her. He failed to realize the good he had done Forty. He was a friend when his neighbor needed one. With his attention focused on what he lost, he missed what he had. He succeeded in keeping his childhood friend alive.

Absentmindedly, he followed them outside without taking a thing, then suddenly remembered the note on the floor. He hurried back in to get it, with Shep and Freckles close at his heels. The car started up and, as he dashed to the front door to see what was going on, Forty drove away, taking himself and the nurse on to the rest home. Tucker sensed a heavy door slammed shut in his face. He was not to take part in whatever would happen next with Forty, as the Chevy convertible, with the top down, drove away in a cloud of dust, the nurse holding on to her hat.

The dogs sat patiently looking up at him, waiting for his next move. Tucker spotted the piece of paper under the edge of the sofa, quickly snatched it up, locked the front door, and left, the dogs running merrily alongside.

He stopped at his house only long enough to pack a few things. What he needed to do next, he thoroughly dreaded, telling himself it was necessary, because where he needed to go in search of Sylvia, the dogs could not go, too.

"Obviously, no one else is going to look for Sylvia, not even her own husband!"

He closed his satchel, whistled to the dogs, and set off once more.

"I'll look for her myself," he proudly announced to no one, though he believed it so loud, the whole town rang with the news.

CHAPTER SEVENTEEN

He dropped his suitcase and scooped up the puppy right as her protective mother tore out of the barn and began to fight with Shep. They were barking, growling, and snapping, the female dog tearing into Shep with a viciousness Tucker had not expected. The fur across the ridge of her back stood on end. Angry and shouting, the blacksmith turned a hose on the two dogs. Tucker held onto Freckles and watched, seeing he made a big mistake in bringing Shep. Fortunately, with the hose spraying the dogs with water, the blacksmith got the female under control and locked her in a stall with her puppies. Shep ignored the man ordering him to go home, so they tied a length of rope to Shep's collar. Finally, the blacksmith's son took the dog home.

Things quieted down afterward. Not knowing what else to do or say, except to apologize, Tucker stood in place holding Freckles. The blacksmith said that Shep was the father of the pups, but "ol' Tessie," refused to allow him near. They fought continuously until Jim separated them. Freckles wiggled and wriggled and whined to be let down, so Tucker set her down. She immediately bounded over to the stall and squeezed through the rails.

Tucker wondered if, or how much, the blacksmith knew about Jim and Sylvia. It was not a topic easily discussed. Hoping to explain why he brought the dogs there, he did say Sylvia Sumner had gone missing, having left without a word. Her husband, Forty, went to stay at the rest home. Secretly hoping the older man might know something and tell him, Tucker was careful to avoid mentioning his own personal interest in the matter. No sooner did he say that he called the sheriff and saw a coroner drive through their neighborhood, when the boy came running up the path with Shep, crying and yelling. He was repeating something awful. The blacksmith strode over to hold him, worried and concerned over the boy's words Tucker strained to understand, when it became suddenly clear.

"Jim's dead! Jim's dead!"

The boy's story spilled out in-between sobs, trying to catch his breath. Shep pulled on the makeshift leash to go over to Tucker, standing next to the barn. Cautiously, Tucker took the leash from the boy. The blacksmith and his son hurriedly closed up shop for the day. Tucker wondered how people know what to do under such sudden and unexpected circumstances. People seem to automatically act, he thought, drawn toward one another, pulling together to share in their loss.

He remembered hearing similar words when his brother, Dewey, died, killed by his own hand, having shot himself. Tucker and his father were the only ones left in the family home after that. They barely talked to one another, not knowing how to get past the senselessness and trauma of the incident, he supposed. He remembered his father was inconsolable, though Tucker heard him pleading with Howard one night in his study, wanting to know why or what went wrong. Howard's wife, Mary, put her arm around his father and hugged him. Tears ran from her eyes unabashedly, but his father's eyes were dry.

Despite Tucker's brief, yet profound recollections, they did little to aid his sense of helplessness in the moment.

The blacksmith and his son quickly drove away to tell everyone they knew. Jim was dead. A murder investigation, swiftly carried out, demanded everyone in town cooperate with the authorities. In reality, the deputies at Jim's house told the boy something more like, "conducting a routine investigation" and "notifying his wife." These official-sounding words soon turned into, "Jim's been murdered and they think his wife did it!"

Tucker remained in shock and disbelief, his mouth yet agape ever since he first realized what the boy had been yelling, "Jim's dead!" Jim was dead and Sylvia was gone. Did she know? Where was Beth? In the moment, he had no answers, but it all came to him then, Shep showing up at Forty's house, the coroner driving down the road, the unfamiliar sheriff's car, the deputy not looking at him, not stopping to talk to him—

"Oh, no!" Tucker said aloud in a state of sudden panic, not knowing what he should do. He told the officer *everything*, He sounded like a guilty man, a jealous man, the deputy said. Giving his testimony in a court of law, his suspicious activities, his spying and jealousy, pinned the guilt on him.

Shep jumped on him with muddy paws, shaking Tucker out of his panic. The hose left on, they were standing in a growing puddle of water. He turned off the water spigot and tugged on the leash.

"Come on, Shep," He picked up his suitcase and took the dog away.

Believing himself friendless, with not a one to whom he could turn, he sought out his family. He hurried up the dirt road that eventually met up with pavement and walked over to Fig Tree Lane. One hand gripped the makeshift leash, the other carried his suitcase. Walking down the shaded street, shook up and rattled, he wanted to be with people he knew, people he loved and who loved him. The house he grew up in, appeared ahead on his left. In stately grace, he always imagined, painted entirely white, except for its green shutters. A large elm tree grew out front surrounded by lawn, the only greenery, except for some withering and stunted geraniums. A massive rose bramble clambered up onto the roof. His oldest brother, Howard, had done well in restoring and maintaining the family home. He knew his brother could be counted on to help. Heading up the front walkway, Tucker practiced giving his brother the news.

Evening drew in on that long day and, like rippling waves and jolts from an earthquake, it sent news of Jim's death reverberating throughout the entire community. Howard got home from work, not having heard the news, but Mary heard it from someone at the drugstore and, "wasn't it awful his own wife murdered him?"

"That can't be!" Tucker reacted impulsively, surprised in his defense of Beth Hart. Seeing Mary turn to her husband in her own defense, he regretted his actions.

She looked up at Howard and meekly reaffirmed the news being passed around town. "A detective is questioning everyone."

Howard asked Mary what exactly they said. They soon discovered the only firmly established and obvious truth, that Jim Hart died. An insurance salesman, Howard gently admonished his wife, telling her, "Now, dear, an investigation is standard procedure. It doesn't mean Jim Hart was murdered by anyone. It's required."

Thus put in her place without another word, a smile of serene bliss returned to Mary's contented life. "Would you like some dinner?" She asked no one in particular.

Tucker infrequently visited his brother and sister-in-law. In his opinion, they led shallow lives, floating off in a dreamworld made of niceties and good manners. Nevertheless, his somewhat cruel judgement of his only brother left living, affected him deeply. He felt ashamed, especially when he walked past their bedroom and saw Howard in his brown suit, holding his wife in his arms, lovingly apologizing for embarrassing her in front of Tucker.

Shep whined loudly, straining at the leash, reminding Tucker he needed them to watch the dog while he carried out his own investigation. It frightened him that, since Sylvia's disappearance coincided with Jim's death, she may be suspected of wrongdoing. Tucker's sense of responsibility toward her grew all of a sudden, when he recalled telling the deputy about Sylvia and Jim's affair. The weather too warm for eating or cooking indoors, Howard volunteered to barbecue hamburgers in the backyard where Shep ran loose. A chainlink fence surrounded it now, "to keep deer out of Grandma's garden," Howard told Tucker.

Surprisingly happy, the dog ran everywhere, sniffing every bush and exploring every pathway in the enormous, half-acre yard. Tucker needed time to reach a serious decision regarding Sylvia, so he let it go, visiting with family like nothing bothered him. They neglected to inquire why Tucker brought Jim's dog. Tucker thought about that himself, only able to conclude it involved a combination of circumstance, and something else.

The way Shep looked at Tucker, following him around, gave him the impression the dog chose him.

With such serious thoughts on his mind, he helped spread the tablecloth on the picnic table, set out the mayonnaise and bowl of potato chips, watched his brother making hamburger patties, while the charcoal briquettes burned into a glowing bed of coals. He observed, how life had to go on despite Death's visit to their beloved little town. Yet, guilt plagued him, thinking he should be joining all those gathering together to mourn their onetime hero. Who those people might be, Tucker never took the opportunity to learn.

Jim's mother, Candelaria, worked in the orchards and, some years ago, moved into the farmworker's housing, after Jim's father died. The Henry's lived up the mountain and mostly kept to themselves. Jim worked very hard in school, Tucker clearly remembered, working to "dig myself out of the ditch my old man dragged our family down into," he overheard Jim telling another teammate. A hero to the students at their high school, and to the community, Jim led the team to victory in their senior year. Unnoticed, once graduation passed and their high school lives receded into the closet with the football, the team jacket, and the yearbooks, was the continued presence of their town hero, supposedly going away to college. He never did that. Tucker remembered all the talk and the cheering, but Jim never left.

An upwelling of compassion rose within him, from his gut where jealousy long brewed, up to his throat, where he halted it. He pretended to be going to see what Shep found, walking away, keeping his back to his brother. Grief choked to the surface, though tears could barely fall. When he found Shep, he knelt down before the dog. Forgetful of his fear of the dog's sharp teeth, he stroked its neck, running his hand across the dog's fur, only then sobbing and regretting terribly he did not befriend Jim in school. Instead, he tormented him.

He closed his eyes and muttered, "I'm sorry, Jim!"

Mary came out the back door with a platter of lettuce leaves and tomato and onion slices, carrying it over to the table, before returning to the house. Reassured his brother and sister-in-law were occupied, Tucker gazed toward the west at the lowering sun. Searching the sky for a message, he listened carefully for what he hoped would soon come his way, and it did. Sometimes lessons come late in life, too late it seems, at times, but through the pain such important lessons strive to teach, one learns and grows as well. He knew this to be true, dwelling so on the past, knowing something profound awaited him, something he almost saw arising from out of his pain.

•　•　•

Fortunate in life, Tucker was loved and cared for in his childhood, growing up to become carefree and happy-go-lucky. That he lacked friends, a wife, and felt unhappy and lonely, at times, he brought that on himself. His heart set on Sylvia, throughout his life, prevented connection to others, mainly women. He resolved this time, not to let her go in the sense he expected to walk away from her and out of her life, when he recently determined to love her. Letting go of her meant, whatever she did, no matter how she lived and loved in her life, he promised to strive toward the same compassion he now experienced for Jim. He resolved to be a better person, to bring the truth out into the sun for all to see.

CHAPTER EIGHTEEN

A thorough examination of Jim Hart's body concluded Friday night. He would not be spending the weekend in a church with loved ones gathered around, but in a cooler with the bodies of those he never met in life, except one. Sylvia's father, "identity unknown," arrived on Friday as well.

"Some bum," they said, "found dead in an alley, gunshot to the head."

The examiner sighed deeply, because he dreaded another unrecognizable face, whole pieces sheared away from the bullet's swift pathway through human tissue and bone. Uncovering him, he relaxed, seeing only a bullet hole. Unfortunately, this one required more paperwork and needed to be held until an investigation helped reveal its story. A hole in the forehead only meant one thing. It was not suicide. The examiner shook his head, pitying the man whose life ended in such a manner. He always wondered where their families were, if anyone cared. After all, he sighed again, this man was somebody's brother, or husband, or someone's father.

The other one who came in the same day, the young man, he was an easy suicide. The examiner's vocabulary did not include the word, "accident." He did not believe in accidents. Everything happened due to a specific cause. The young man's blood alcohol level measured high enough, to have killed him, all by itself. The examiner concluded, this man wanted to die. "Why else would he leave his clothes on? Because, he intended to kill himself, that's why," chuckling over what his grandchildren often said, "accidentally on purpose."

Despite what his findings needed to show in a report, the examiner knew the real cause of death, not only when he read the report accompanying the body, but when he first saw the young man's face.

He said aloud to himself, as though talking to someone there, "Passed-out drunk in a bathtub after his wife leaves him and what shows on his face? Peace, absolute peace."

It was simple. Nevertheless, his report could not contain his opinion and rationale, only his findings, and he wrote: "Suicide." Filling out the rest of the particulars on the form, he then filed it away along with the others. He received a phone call from the detective on the case, answered all of his questions, and that was it. Not until Monday, would anything else be done. He shut out the light, closed the door, and went home with another week gone, another Friday finally over.

The detective left his office, soon driving the interstate homeward. The examiner informed him over the phone before he left, that he found no evidence of a struggle, no marks on the victim's body. He called it a definite suicide, adding that drowning was the primary cause of death, with extreme alcohol intoxication as a significant, contributing factor. The detective radioed the two deputies who were guarding Jim's house and told them to go on home. "No one's gonna bother that house."

Already, carelessness set in, a habit that grew the more years he spent at his thankless job. He covered up his blindspot with the pretense of caring at the start of his shift, but which played itself out by the end of his shift. Once a good detective, his performance slid downward over the years into good enough, then barely passable. Fortunately, a few, positive elements remained that kept him going and kept him employed.

Thinking over what he accomplished that day, he quickly patted his shirt pocket, checking on a notepad he hastily stowed. A loose string of notes, absentmindedly jotted down, he judged, added up to a whole lot of nothing. That was about it. Sure, the examiner told him, "a definite suicide," but it occurred in a roundabout sort-of-way. This particular case aroused his curiosity. He wanted to know why the dead man's dog showed up at Sumner's house, the man who reported his wife missing. No one he asked seemed to know any of the answers to his questions, but he was familiar with these rural town folks, loyal to one another. Well, he thought, as he shook his head in disgust and turned down the street on which he lived, even the sheriff's deputy hid something. He determined to get to the bottom of it. He secretly longed to do something to revive his lackluster career, to generate some interest in his job again.

In the mean time, a surprising bit of information may prove useful. The deputy recovered an old gun from Sumner, who accidentally shot himself with it one night, two months ago. He read the whole report. Now, the detective found it of particular interest. Concrete proof the deputy knew something, the detective nodded his head.

"First thing, Monday morning," he told himself, "I'm going to pay ol' Deputy Carson a little visit in his out-of-the-way substation."

Swinging onto his driveway, home at last, he set aside thoughts from work for the weekend. One last idea held his attention before he shut off the engine, his reason for continuing the investigation, to follow-up on the woman reported missing. He ascertained her part in this story provided an important clue in connection with Jim Hart's tragic end. Using his fingers, he tallied-off each item to address on Monday.

"Question Hart's co-workers and the missing woman's husband. Then, head over to the substation. After that? We'll see what comes next."

• • •

Earlier in the day, before her husband's death, Beth left their house seeking revenge. Anger consumed her, feeding off her own unresolved pain and suffering. Out of her misery, she transformed into a bitter, hateful woman, one given to streaks of meanness and pure cruelty. Tufts of hair coiled out from her head, like live, venomous snakes. She painted once again a startling vision of virulent passion, as on that evening past, when she and her husband confronted Tucker behind their house.

Approaching the Sumner's home, she slowed her car. No sign of anyone at home, her plan already began to falter. She arrived much later than she and Sylvia arranged. Beth hoped Sylvia might yet be waiting, not having any transportation of her own. They were to visit the priest, Father Jovial, then go to the bus stop out on the highway, where Sylvia would depart.

However, Beth had additional plans of her own for "that husband stealer."

She parked the car in the driveway, got out and assailed the front door with her pounding. No one answered. Through cupped hands placed against the front windowpane, her pinched scowl beheld an empty home. Sylvia was gone, though a pack of cigarettes lay on the coffee table. Beth refused to submit to defeat. She grabbed the doorknob, turning, twisting, and pulling, trying to yank the door open. Repeatedly banging her fist on the door, it held fast against her venting anger and frustration. The wood of the door's aged panels would not cave in to her kicking feet and foul oaths spewing from her betrayed heart.

Her yellow Chrysler carried all she owned. A few belongings in a paper sack, a box of odds and ends, lay ignored, along with the future, about which she could strive to do differently. Though, her bitterness gave rise to a narrowed view that saw only a crushed and defeated plan laying in waste before her. One, last, childish vow, she hurled with a swift kick into the sturdy wooden door.

"I'll get you someday! I'm not gonna let you get away with ruining my marriage!

CHAPTER NINETEEN

Kneeling before the priest in a posture of humility, her hands folded in front of her, Sylvia confessed to him her sins. She told the priest of her long-term secret relationship with Jim Hart, her wish to annul her marriage, and her decision to search for her father.

Father Jovial moved to their valley long before Edenville became established. He helped build their church. He knew Sylvia's parents since they were born. He visited his parishioners and knew what went on in their homes. What he told her, as her head lowered to receive the palm of his hand in blessing, was drawn from all those years.

"Child," he began, because he was himself over ninety years of age and quite gray with teary, old eyes, "God knows all."

His voice was kind and he chose his words carefully. They were not going to be stock phrases he gave many of his parishioners in confession, because not only did he know Sylvia's story, he knew her heart, her soul, through all the years. He sensed, somehow, and he believed it was the Lord speaking to him, she was at a turning point in her life. God told him exactly what he should say to her. So, he went on.

"He sees all that happens in life and He has a wonderful plan for each and every one of us. It was the right thing to end this relationship you had with young Mr. Hart, but no need to fret or worry. You see, the Lord has already forgiven you. Your wish to annul your marriage will be granted, but it will take time. Now, because of your acceptance of what God has in store for you, you will embark on an important journey. You wish to find your father. The Lord will send divine guidance to aid you in this matter. He will also place within you the strength to forgive him, as the Lord has forgiven you. He knows your heart, child, and He knows it is a good heart. May the Lord bless you," and Father Jovial's shaky hand raised before her as he motioned the Sign of the Cross, "in the name of the Father, the Son, and the Holy Ghost. Amen."

•   •   •

Sylvia's mother and father were poor. Aunt Justice lived within her meager means of support. Though Sylvia had a way with money, when it came to providing herself and Fortuitous with nice clothes, her life with him was, for the most part, plain and simple as well. Except a day at the county fair her aunt participated in each and every year, they never took any trips. Aunt Justice won blue ribbons for her handmade dresses, so Sylvia's wardrobe, at least while growing up, contained handmade, award winners. Once married, she purchased their clothes through the mail-order catalogs at the clothing store located in the shopping center. Never had she seen, nor felt the need to see the world beyond their small valley, except those annual days at the fair when she was a girl.

Seated on the bus, the world she knew slipped away in a blur as she looked timidly around at her fellow travelers. Wondering where they had been and where they were going, she noticed how different they were from the people she knew. One group, wearing tie-dyed shirts and leather sandals, with colorful beads clattering as they hopped from seat to seat, were what she knew as hippies, behaving like playful children. She behaved so proper and reserved in comparison to everyone else on the bus. Somewhere in her, laughter abounded, such as Tucker had known. This laughter erupted like an unexpected burp, when a pet bird flew from one of the hippie's shoulders over to the top of her head. He got up from his seat to retrieve it.

"Rooster! Get back here!"

Holding still, while he gently scooped the little flit of feathers from her head, Sylvia was instantly delighted with Rooster, a small, yellow, white, and orange cockatiel. Its owner, eager to break the boredom of a monotonous bus trip, sat next to her and began to talk. The other hippies, of which all seemed to be friends with one another, gathered around. One began to play a guitar.

One of the girls wore a loose-fitting dress, kneeling on the seat ahead, facing toward them. Her braless-ness brought a word to Sylvia's mind, "flouncing," and she instantly looked away out the window. She became surrounded by adult-sized kindergarteners, she thought, wanting to see inside her purse, studying her brooch. The man seated next to her shooed them away. They scattered to other quiet passengers whom, they remarked, were much too serious.

Sylvia long ago learned of her effect on men. Her fine taste in dress and décor, her careful poise, created an illusion upon first impression, that she belonged to that elite class of people who traveled the world and were photographed arriving at galas and banquets. Her face was clear and admirably flawless. Her black hair, shiny, like a pool of water in the moon's soft light, she kept styled in a precise cut, somewhat of a bob.

Her sad, gray eyes compelled the man to sit by her, certain that, at last, he found someone interesting and intelligent with whom he could engage in conversation. They exchanged names, his being Andrew. He shared that he traveled by bus across the country and back, participating in protests against the war. He politely inquired of her own reasons for traveling, adding, "I mean, this is beautiful country. Why would you want to leave it?"

He sat low in the seat, so his head rested on the back of it. The bird tugged on strands of his golden-streaked, brown hair. He wore it long, curling up from under the bandanna tied around his head, then over his ears, down to almost his shoulders. The guitar played on and another song emanated from out of the fading background, experienced as everywhere but right where the two of them, Andrew and Sylvia, now sat.

Occasionally, the bird pecked at the lenses of the man's wire-rimmed glasses. Sylvia tried to suppress a grin, though failed, unable to be serious enough to answer his question. She had to look away to keep from laughing. Her mirth surprised her, until the fact of their delightful, mutual attraction for one another dawned on her. Once this was established, she had no trouble remaining serious. She gauged him to be around her same age, maybe older. His mustache grew down along the sides of his mouth, toward his chin. She noticed his general physical appearance, combined with his age, differed from the hippies she usually encountered. What she discerned through intuition, his self-expression related to his passion, protesting the war, telling others wherever he went, "I am not afraid to tell you who I am!"

Plainly as could be, she answered his question, "I'm going to look for my father."

"What?"

"I'm going to look for my father," she repeated.

"Wow. When was the last time you saw him?"

He seemed genuinely interested. His concerned expression, looking directly at her, and the intimate manner in which he behaved toward her, impressed Sylvia, but also touched upon her weakness. Temptation struck again. Clearly, she announced in her mind, God was testing her. Imagining herself sliding down in the seat to make an already-tempting intimacy even more tempting, she became determined to fight it by speaking only of her father. No need for Father Jovial's statement on the importance of her quest. She wanted that to be why she rode on the bus out into the world for the first time, yet reminded herself, the priest said God would send divine guidance to aid her.

"I haven't seen him since I was . . . just a girl." She hesitated, because she truly could not remember when she last saw him.

Her eyes grew more sad and, as she looked out the window, the man hesitated continuing the discussion, wondering what he should do. He met many types of people on his cross-country trip, some of them to whom he regretted speaking. Seated close enough to her, he felt the warmth of her skin against his own, he chose to stay beside her. He liked her very much. Intuition being a gift with him, he sensed in her a rarity, neurotic, yes, but intriguing, and not at all dangerous. He mused, imagining himself stepping into a nineteenth-century novel set in England.

No one on the bus knew he used to be an English professor at a well-known university. He left his profession to live life as nearest the source and his true nature as he could possibly achieve. He long desired to become a playwright or even a screenwriter. Here, Sylvia entered into his life, a woman not like any he ever met. She inspired him.

Andrew never fit into the college scene, frustrated with the politics that made even the best of friends amongst his colleagues, turn into the bitterest of enemies. His traveling companions were people whom he met earlier that day, who attached themselves to him. They were much younger than himself, none other than the same group of young people Sylvia's husband met earlier in the week. They were not traveling cross-country, merely across the county, their bus tickets purchased with the money they received selling Forty's old comic books.

When the bus arrived at a city, which happened to be the county seat, the group of young hippies, minus the one man, traipsed and danced off the bus without any luggage. This was Sylvia's stop, more than sixty miles from home. She rose with purse and suitcase, one in each hand, and stood close to him. She quietly thanked him when he stepped back to let her go first, then moved along slowly, glancing back at him. He pulled his own bag from the rack above and followed closely behind her. Having engaged him through her body language, Sylvia encouraged Andrew, though her manner was sheer habit, about which she no longer held any awareness. Although married, having only recently disavowed herself from a lover, she feared finding her father and what the discovery would entail. She must face him, she told herself, well-aware of her compulsion to run away. In spite of her anxiety, Sylvia was unable to run anymore.

From the bus stop, they walked together, working their way through a small crowd of people in line to get on the bus. The young hippies hailed him, "Andrew!" He merely waved to them to say goodbye. Having gotten off the bus miles from his destination, which they knew, they assumed he must be joining them. Disappointed he was not, they climbed into the car of a friend picking them up, and drove away.

Sylvia skipped eating lunch, but it was too early for dinner. Father Jovial directed her to this particular city, because he knew Robert Cadwallader worked as a janitor for the county hospital. They might know where he lives. First, she needed to get a hotel room, but warned herself not to mention it to Andrew, to wait until they parted company. Perhaps, she thought, coffee would be safest, looking for her idea of a coffeeshop, one not unlike the country-style diner in her hometown.

She asked Andrew, "Would you mind stopping to get a cup of coffee?"

"No, not at all."

Andrew's idea of a coffeeshop was the coffeehouse where college students congregated and read poetry, talked and argued about the war, listened to jazz or folk music—and he could tell Sylvia was not the coffeehouse type. Even though he criticized the college town atmosphere and all that he judged as the "faddish collection of the times," he did appreciate the occasional, enlightening discussions found in such places. Nevertheless, he chose to get off the bus when Sylvia had, because he wanted, more than anything, to draw her out from the shadows within which he knew she hid. Reaching the older section of town, they eventually found a clean, quiet cafe, neither countrified nor taken over by the counterculture prevailing across the country. Andrew hoped for a quiet place where they could, in all honesty, get to know one another a little better.

They sat down in a booth, soon enjoying a fairly decent cup of coffee, which Sylvia ordered along with toast. She made a mistake, in her mind, to go along with this man with the little bird riding on his shoulder, when she should have shook his hand, told him goodbye, and walked away. Thinking clearly escaped her, for some reason. Her small world of familiarities lay miles back up the highway. Here, she entered into a world of unknowns.

She continually returned to the explanation, God was testing her, though believed she failed. Uncertain about how to correct her mistake, rather than further deepen her failure to adhere to a commitment to change her ways, she fell into small talk. Her rationale being, to overcome her awkwardness, too uncomfortable sitting in silence, and she must find a place to stay the night. Small talk may be her way out of the cafe and on her way, alone.

"So, where do you live?"

Andrew did not do small talk and answered vaguely, "Oh, it's a ways down the road." He perceived Life too grand to reduce to insignificance and brought her back to what interested him most, her search and her sadness. "How do you plan to find someone you haven't seen in—how old did you say you were?"

"Thirty . . . one." Sylvia momentarily pulled away from their conversation, realizing her birthday came and went without gifts, and she missed seeing Jim.

Andrew noticed Sylvia's withdrawal, slightly ashamed of his curiosity he feared may be out of place and inappropriate. In an attempt to apologize, all he managed to say, was, "I'm—I shouldn't have—" He left it at that.

Both silent, neither were able to walk away from the other.

Pondering their attraction for one another, Sylvia also experienced Andrew's closeness, while sitting together on the bus. Out of the discomfort of not knowing what to do, she ventured looking into his eyes from across their booth, a brown color so light, they appeared golden. She liked this man. She fancied them standing side by side at the edge of a cliff overlooking an unforeseeable future, the only knowing possible, to take each other's hand and leap.

"A friend," she was referring to Father Jovial, "told me my father had worked at the county hospital once. He said they might know where he is." A secondary discomfort, resulting from the subject of their conversation, a subject she never talked about with anyone throughout most of her life, caused her heart to race. Under the table, in her lap, she rubbed the palms of her hands together and struggled to calm herself. Suddenly, as though controlled by unseen forces, Sylvia got up to leave.

"I'm sorry. I need to—"

She picked up her purse and suitcase and hurried out, cheeks reddening in an obvious blush. As she stood on the sidewalk, feeling anxious, overwhelming uncertainty crowded into her awareness and left her confused.

Andrew quickly paid for the coffee and toast and left the cafe to join her. She began to walk away from him, so he followed along beside her, even though she kept looking away. He reached out to touch her arm and said, "Please, let me help you." He could tell she was in need of a friend.

She stopped and closed her eyes, sighing, but answered, "All right."

With his own belongings slung across his back in an old and faded knapsack, they walked together to find some lodging. Truly relieved, though disappointed in herself she could not, or would not do other than to let him help. Outwardly, her poise and graceful movements hid her fear and nervousness.

They appeared to be an unlikely pair, his long hair and faded jeans alongside her elegant appearance. But, Andrew and Sylvia walked beside one another as equals. They were traveling companions of the soul, having joined together, sharing in something important of which neither of them were fully aware.

Soon, they entered into the historical district, comprised of restored, historical businesses and homes. Andrew pointed to a small, old-west-style hotel down the street, called, "The Six-Gun Retreat & Bath House," advertising baths for a nickel and rooms for fifty-cents. Probably a tourist trap, he thought.

"That one looks nice," and Sylvia made her choice.

She hurried across the street with Andrew. Up the stairs and down the narrow hallway, every floor board crackling or creaking underfoot, their rooms were soon located. The moment she entered her room and the door was shut, she set down her suitcase on the lumpy brass bed and covered her face with her hands. Andrew's room was next to her own. Hearing a slight thump, she quickly withdrew her hands and turned her head to listen. She pictured him merely dropping his knapsack from his shoulders to the floor, secretly hoping to share a room with him. She knew Andrew also hoped for the same. Other things to consider, told her to wait and see.

She fought with her own advice, standing at the door to her room, her hand on the doorknob, wanting to go to him. Her internal argument covered the reasons why she should or should not do so. Feeling nauseous, she placed the palm of her hand on her abdomen, reminded of—and let go of the doorknob as though it had become burning hot.

Pacing the floor of her room, her worrisome thoughts returned to Jim. She wondered what happened. She admitted to herself she thought it best to end their affair, but postponed doing so, because she believed she would miss him more than she could bear. In her deeper fears, she foretold he would hurt himself. What became painfully clear to her long before Tucker spied her going to his house, formulated from out of an encounter with Jim's darker side.

He let slip a fearful side of himself, a flash of anger while gripping her arm, telling her the strangest thing. She only mentioned Tucker's name and he yanked her close to him, "I don't *ever* want to hear you say his name again! *Got it?!*"

There were other instances. Before Easter, he always apologized and made it up to her, but not anymore.

"It's over," she whispered.

Away from him and her old familiar surroundings, she took a deeper look at her life and why she spent so much of it involved with such a troubled man. Freeing, at first, escaping her husband, but freedom dissolved into an angry face once Jim showed that dangerous side of himself. She noticed other things about him and their relationship, which she missed recognizing when they first appeared, disturbing things. They caused her to wonder if she became his property. Years of her life spent, devoted to a man whom she now admitted, turned selfish, no longer giving her anything in return. She belonged to him and the freedom she once imagined she ran toward, fell into illusion.

Her life of running away ceased to exist. Now, she prepared herself to face the pain she spent nearly a lifetime struggling to overcome. She had not overcome anything, she now knew. She only learned well how to pretend the loss of her mother, where it all began, did not frighten her. Facing the truth, she allowed it to overcome *her*, feeling herself become lightly awash with sadness long-denied. Grief presided too long over her life, grief as a result of the impoverished existence with her emotionally absent father, Aunt Justice, and Fortuitous. Here was a man very different from all the men she ever knew, who did not take advantage of her. Hearing the cockatiel, Rooster, calling out occasionally, her thoughts were broken and she simply stepped out of her room and over to his.

She knocked on his door, but no answer came. She returned to her room, changed her clothes, and set out for some sightseeing. Walking through Olde Towne, looking for a good place to eat, lifted her mood. Admiring various window displays, she discovered a dress shop, "From the Heart," which appealed to her. She browsed through the racks, receiving a compliment on her hair style by its owner. The woman told her she needed to hire someone to help her out in the shop.

"I never get a day off. Always working, working." She then perked up, "Say! How would you like to work here? You've got good taste! Anybody can see that."

She waited for Sylvia's reply, but she only said, "Oh, I couldn't . . ."

The woman told her to think about it. Sylvia agreed. The woman gave her a business card, saying, "Call me if you change your mind."

Smiling, Sylvia left the shop and continued to walk down the sidewalk, when she caught sight of Andrew across the street. She almost called his name, about to hurry across to greet him, but she hesitated. It appeared someone threw him out of a store, probably its owner, whom he argued with out on the sidewalk.

The shopkeeper pointed his finger threateningly toward Andrew, saying, "It's because of people like you this country's going down the toilet!"

Andrew argued in return, "We shouldn't be in Vietnam! The government's brainwashed everybody, telling them that we're fighting Communism, but we're really butting in where we don't belong!"

"You damn hippie! Why don't you run off to Canada with all your type? Who needs you?! Let the real men fight this war— and we're gonna win, too!"

"You don't even understand what's really going on in that country!"

"Shut up, you damn Commie! And stay the hell away from my store!"

Sylvia was in a state of shock, witnessing Andrew and the life he led. Men in her town often argued over politics, but no one took the side Andrew had taken. It shook her out of her small-town, protective enclosure. Andrew saw her and ran across the street, knowing she had been observing his argument with the shopkeeper.

"Sylvia! Are you all right?!" Without thinking, he hugged her close to him.

She tried to think of what to say, but nothing came to mind. No words could reach her and she reeled, holding her forehead, nearly faint. Andrew walked with her to her room, got her some water, and had her lay down. His kindness, his soothing voice as he stroked her hair, surprisingly reminded her of Tucker and she began wishing he was there with her. He knew her better than anyone and she missed him in her life. Tucker had been her very best friend and, as this stranger treated her with kindness, she now longed to—

"Who is he?"

She was confused by Andrew's question. "What do you mean?"

"The man you're thinking about right now. What's his name?"

"How do you know what I'm thinking about?"

"Come on. Who is he?"

He laid himself down beside her, holding onto her hand and continuing to gently stroke her hair as she told him.

"Tucker. Tucker Stewart."

A lumpy mattress never felt so soft, nor the sun, streaming through the dusty lacework of curtains, so reassuring. Andrew gazed upon her, his eyes looking all about her face and, for the first time, she lay beside a man in bed and felt absolutely at peace with herself. She returned his gaze and, a smile growing on her face, she almost knew—

"You're not going to find your father, Sylvia."

A sudden upwelling of tears caught her off guard. She asked him, "How do you know?"

"I'm not sure. But, I think it's Tucker you need now. And he needs you."

•   •   •

The following morning was Saturday. Personnel offices at the county hospital were closed until Monday. They would not even give her the phone number of someone in personnel, nothing. Sylvia recalled what Andrew told her. Disappointed and nearly heartbroken, she remembered his striking, golden eyes. Looking out the front windows of the hospital lobby, arms folded in front of her, her thoughts drifted from Andrew to Tucker.

A maintenance man, with keys jingling and pace in a morning rush, asked Sylvia if she could move out of his way. He wanted to hurry and get his overtime in before the ballgame started on television.

"Excuse me."

She was oblivious.

"Excuse me, Miss. I need to—"

"Oh! I'm sorry!"

She hastily stepped aside while he wheeled his trashcan past, emptying ash trays, picking up shriveled balls of used tissue, and dumping out waste baskets, straightening rugs. He set about washing handprints from the front windows. Maybe sixty years old, Joaquin Mendoza was one of Jim's uncles and her father's long-time friend.

It occurred to Sylvia he might know her father, so she asked, "You wouldn't happen to know a Robert Cadwallader, would you?"

His face lit up with a smile, answering "Oh, Caddie? Sure, I know Caddie." He sprayed the window here and there and began to briskly wipe each spot dry. "What do you want to know?"

"I'm his daughter. I was looking for him and someone told me he worked here."

"His daughter?!" The man was surprised, quickly shaking his head, as though to rattle himself awake from a dream, and stood there as the window spray dripped down the glass. "His daughter?" He repeated it again as though disbelieving it the first time.

"Yes. Would you know where he might be? Does he still work here?"

He went back to wiping the glass clean and dry. "Well . . ." He was reluctant to say, stopping his work again as he grew very serious, unfolding and then refolding his towel. "He doesn't work here anymore. He got too sick," pointing to his stomach, "you know, from drinking too much. His liver. Real bad." He slowly and thoughtfully wiped the last spot on the glass, "But, you know," he turned to her, looked around to see who else was there and lowered his voice, "He's been missing. Nobody's seen him for two, three days." He shook his head again, saying, "It's not good," as he prepared to move on with his work. Before he did so, he thought she looked very sad and disappointed, so went on, "He never said anything about a daughter. He was always—" Looking down, he nodded his head, agreeing with what he mentally decided, then looked up at her again. "He's missing," and his arms went up in a gesture of defeat and "what can be done?" He wanted to be of more help to her, but, "No one knows where he is. If you want to find him, you be careful. He knew some bad people."

His voice trailed away, because Sylvia's mind wandered. The next thing she knew, a slip of paper appeared in front of her, the man having written down the address of where her father lived, a trailer park in the town nearest her own. He lived closer to her than she thought. She thanked the man and returned to her hotel room to tell Andrew all she learned, but he was gone.

CHAPTER TWENTY

Saturday morning and the highway absolutely empty, Tucker stopped momentarily to appreciate the rare occasion. He habitually noted seasonal differences in traffic flow, being a gifted observer, though some might call it nosiness. In winter, a steady stream of cars passed through, on their way up to ski resorts and steaming mugs of hot chocolate next to a stone fireplace. He always imagined it that way, though he never saw such places, except on television. In summer, which had not yet arrived, campers and fishermen filled the roadway. Currently in-between seasons, the backcountry roads affected by winter closures, very few vehicles drove through, mostly locals.

To his left, heading west, the shopping center lay nearby and, a little ways beyond, the old roadhouse hung on to its life. The highway continued straight west, up out of the valley and then over a rise, a few miles from where he stood. To his right, heading east, the highway took drivers up into the higher mountain regions. In this direction, it left the valley at a steep grade, steadily rising in elevation not far from where he stood. Pine Way Junction, the backroad he often walked, met the highway about a half a mile in that direction from where he currently stood. An unpaved road, primarily used by locals, took drivers southward. It steadily climbed, made a wide arc through scenic natural areas, before returning to the oldest part of town where Tucker lived in the original Stewart home. That was his street, so little used by locals anymore, the county threatened to abandon it. The little town to which it led barely survived. Tucker found comfort in the fact that the real old-timers still referred to his end of the valley as Pine Way.

The rest home sat directly across the highway, at the bottom of Spring Hill. It demonstrated classical architecture at its finest, very stately, though very green. Tucker knew for a fact it was apple green, of which he obtained surplus cans to paint his house. Volunteering his time to help paint the rest home was worth it, though he would have preferred a nice cream color. Reasons for maintaining a green exterior for the rest home were many. Mostly, according to the maintenance man, "Rest homes are always painted green."

He walked across the highway, hesitating before proceeding toward the front entrance. He never knew what kind of day his father was having. A good day meant he did not fuss or lose his temper with anyone, and he cooperated with the nurses. A bad day meant the medication they gave him caused a reaction, or he spit it up, or a myriad of other reasons reminding Tucker of his grandfather. Little wonder his grandpa passed away soon after his symptoms got so bad he could no longer feed himself. Dubious of whether it did any good, Tucker and his brother agreed their father would receive treatment. Although, pills and nursing care constituted said treatment, going on three years now.

When it first began, Tucker respected their decision, confident it was best for his father. Now that he knew of the sad days, three years seemed a long time for one's father to slowly die. Neither good days nor bad, the conditions in which he witnessed his father languish, became most evident. Tucker sat at a distance, watching a nurse try to feed his father, head shaking up and down, side to side. Looking away did little to improve the view. He could see into other rooms where the other residents were having similarly sad days. Tucker prayed not to end up like that. A strange, sour odor to the place, oftentimes pervaded the air. He winced and begged to open a window. Howard never went to see their father, never saw what Tucker saw every Tuesday for lunch when he visited. Today was Saturday. He did not know what kind of day this would be.

He reached into his pants pocket for his watch, but it was gone. Quickly, he patted each and every pocket, looking around, seeing it nowhere. Never, in all the years he owned it, had he ever misplaced his watch. He felt lost without it. First, Jim dies, then Sylvia leaves, now this! His predictable, orderly world was erased. A heavy load of concrete, it seemed, took its place, piled onto his shoulders, making him sink to the ground. Eating breakfast later than usual would not have affected him in this way. He sat down under the weight, while tears burning from his chest all the way up his throat met his eyes. They were quickly held in abeyance, for it would do him no good to be in such a state while visiting his father.

Feeling immensely tired, he sat in the early morning coolness. The mountain ridge to the east yet hid the sun, though its warmth would soon arrive.

"I should get a move on," he advised himself, though remained seated.

He kept replaying the words in his memory, "I should get a move on," through a string of repetitive thoughts stuck over and over on, "Jim's dead! Jim's dead!"

The boy's face, unforgettable, his eyes wide, and the blacksmith springing into action, close up the barn, drive away, go tell everyone. He wondered if Sylvia knew. Where was she, but gone off somewhere, while Tucker had a burning, gaping emptiness within his heart? It inexplicably weighed as much as a man, a man who once lived and loved, then was no more. Resigned, Tucker stood up and marched inside the building. Sylvia would not be found while he sat and pondered his grief.

His father was getting his bath, so Tucker wandered around the community room. They maintained this space specifically for visitors. Comfortable chairs sat attractively along the walls. Tall windows, shaded outdoors by awnings, allowed in enough light to brighten the room without adding excessive heat. A few houseplants accented the green walls. On holidays, such as Thanksgiving, Christmas, and Easter, tables would be placed for special meals and family visits.

The nurse who called at Forty's house sat behind a desk facing the community room. Tucker slept very little the night before and, he could tell by her face, she had very little as well. He wondered why, tempted to ask. They exchanged hellos. Tucker stopped milling about and merely stood by her desk with his hands in his front pockets, waiting to see his father. Occasionally, he glanced over in her direction.

The nurse kept looking his way, too, wanting to talk to him, and imagining his arms around her, so she could cry on his shoulder. Beth Hart, who came to stay with her, had a horrible disposition and ranted on and on to her all night about Sylvia Sumner. The nurse regretted, miserably, having made such an offer to that woman! She wished she knew beforehand that Beth was such a heavy drinker, though the word, "lush," came to mind. Tucker's presence nearby drove her to distraction. She noticed him watching her stack papers, stapling some, setting them wherever they needed to be set. Looking his way, she imagined leaping from her chair and throwing herself at him.

Now, whereas she thought Forty was kinda cute, she had a thing for Tucker. She recalled when he volunteered to help paint Spring Hill, thrilled to be able to see more of him. Inventing excuses to talk to him, she often brought him a sandwich or a glass of water. He was tall, yet of average build, athletic, but not like some Hercules. She admired tall men and, evidently, liked men whose hair was an indifferent brown, because she envisioned herself running her fingers through it, then down across his chest where she now longed to lay her head. Happily gazing upon his manly form, she sighed. It appeared to her that he was blind to her attraction for him, and went back to her paperwork.

Tucker always trusted this nurse, found her knowledgeable and efficient, not moody or unpredictable, or irritable. And, yes, he liked her, too. This morning, he wanted to ask her if she knew whatever happened to Robert Cadwallader, but also respected her job, not wanting to interrupt her.

She wanted more than anything for him to talk to her, so she could stop pretending to be doing office work, hoping he would notice her. She finally stopped and asked him, "Do you need something?"

"Well, uhh, actually I do." He drew his hands out of his pockets and walked up to her desk and said, "I'm wondering about a man who stayed here a few years ago, if anyone here might know how I can find him."

"What's his name?"

"Cadwallader. Robert Cadwallader."

"Oh."

The nurse looked at him, knowing it was against the rules to give out information about past residents. Ignorant of the fact the man he asked about was Sylvia's father and Tucker was on a quest to find them both, she chose to break the rules. She would do anything for Tucker Stewart. Checking around for other employees, she whispered to him, leaning across the desk toward him. Hand to the side of her mouth, she told him as much as she dared.

"He got a job as a janitor. At the county hospital."

The head nurse walked by and the one speaking with Tucker, straightened herself, grabbed some papers and briskly tidied them.

"I'm sorry, I have to get back to work, but let me know if that helped."

She wanted him to remember her and to know she was a helpful, even companionable person. She told him what he wanted to know and, in so doing, she also *showed* him what she wanted him to know. Tucker's glance down the front of her uniform, when she leaned forward to whisper to him, did not go unappreciated. This nurse thought of herself as very clever. Impressed with his helping out with Forty and that he was a kind, caring man, and loved animals, she decided to move beyond mere admiration of him during his weekly visits. She decided, then and there, to pursue him with everything she had in her power. Tucker was gold to her and she had gold fever.

Her name was Eileen. She never forgot, while at Forty's house, overhearing Forty in his drugged sleep, mumbling something about, "Tucker, you better stay away from my wife," so she knew she needed to move quickly. Twenty-eight years old and unmarried long enough, was how she saw herself. She figured she could help Beth to get her own place, or maybe move to an apartment nearby. Perfect! She would be able to visit with Tucker after hours and on her days off. Cheered by the prospect of a good catch, despite her lack of sleep, she brightened considerably and went about her work. Especially eager for her lunch hour, she anticipated inquiring about vacancies at the Hillview Apartments. Tucker Stewart, she vowed, was not going to be a single man for long.

In the mean time, Tucker walked down a short hallway to his father's room, grinning over his luck. The nurse knew exactly where to begin looking for Sylvia's father. Though anxious to begin his search for Sylvia, another face now held a special place in his mind, that of a very nice, attractive, young nurse. He made a mental note, tacked it up right next to her image, to be sure and thank her.

In his father's room, he saw bath time ended and they brought him his oatmeal. Though Tucker gagged at the thought of it, he sat and soon had his own bowl of thick oatmeal set before him. Pleased with the addition of toast and crispy bacon, he prepared to enjoy his meal. Surprisingly, though he assumed it standard practice for guests at breakfast, a fresh carnation lay on his tray. He thanked the orderly wheeling in trays of food to each room, set his napkin in his lap and smiled. After good-mornings and how-are-you's were exchanged between himself and his father, he set about eating. Hot coffee and orange juice, he discovered, were also placed on his tray, though his father was always given warm milk.

A nurse came in to feed his father, not his favorite nurse and one he was unlucky enough to see. She wiped the oatmeal dripping from his father's chin.

"It's stretching the rules for you to be here so early in the morning."

He decided not to let her ruin what was, moments before, beginning to look like a perfectly good day.

"Well, this is a special visit. Right, Dad?"

His father lifted his hand a bit, meaning, "That's right."

This nurse, whom Tucker often likened to a rhinoceros in those nature shows on television, walked out of the room, mumbling what ought to be done and, if she were in charge, and generally doing as she always did. He knew it was best to ignore it. He began to ramble on about the friendly young nurse he never noticed before and marveled aloud there were still women like that in the world.

"Not that I'm interested in asking her out on a date or anything."

He sipped his coffee and, reading his father's eyes, knew he listened to everything Tucker said.

"Maybe I will ask her out on a date, or at least over for dinner," pleasantly recalling her maneuver, leaning over the desk to whisper to him. He put the Easter ham in the freezer and, thus, needed another note, to thaw out the ham.

Remembering why he visited on a Saturday, Tucker's mood turned serious, the sad facts of life not so easily forgotten.

"Dad?"

His breakfast finished, he wiped his mouth with the napkin. Putting the carnation in a button hole on his shirt pocket, Tucker missed seeing Eileen walk past, smiling his way. He then looked intently at his father, wondering how much he really understood anymore. He had to try.

"Something has happened. Umm . . . I don't know if you remember him, but Jim Hart died yesterday and . . . do you remember Sylvia? Used to live next door to us."

Tucker immediately became frustrated, dropping his hands in his lap. It seemed a futile effort. His father's uncontrollable motions of his head and his hands, his struggle to speak mostly resulting in unintelligible, broken mutterings, further upset him. He went on regardless.

"She married Fortuitous Sumner and, well, she up and left him. I promised her husband I would find her."

In truth, Forty no longer cared whether Sylvia came back. He was going through hell of a different sort, wanting his pain pills and not able to have any. His time there would change him for good. While he admitted to his share of the blame for a failed marriage, anger tormented him and everyone around him. He ignored their suffering.

Forty yelled, "When I get my hands on that Tucker Stewart, *he's a dead man!*"

Convinced once again of Tucker's guilt involving his wife's unfaithfulness, without the pills to reduce him to a needy and whimpering child, Forty hurled threats and called everyone names.

"I need something for pain! Can't you see that, you—"

The length of Forty's stay was left up to him, though they would have liked for him to have already gone. The young nurse who liked Tucker, could no longer bear his yelling. She heard enough from Beth about Sylvia and Tucker. Here, at work, she listened to it again, from Forty. She asked to be placed elsewhere.

Word of Jim's death reached the Spring Hill Residence & Infirmary with the detective's looming shadow. The head nurse told the nurse in charge of one area who told the nurse in charge of another area and, before Friday was over, Forty knew as well. He mourned the loss of a friend who, dare he acknowledge the thought occurred to him, was involved with his wife.

Tucker's father heard the news as well. Continuing to tell his father what he planned to do, to locate Robert Cadwallader and, hopefully, find Sylvia, his father kept doing something strange. He kept looking away. It annoyed Tucker, who neglected to take the time to try and understand what his father meant. It was difficult enough trying to say what he had to say. It got to the point where his frustration grew until he nearly lost his temper and blurted out, "Would you stop that, Dad, and listen to what I'm trying to tell you?!"

Fortunately, those words were never said. Tucker gave up altogether. He sat, hands folded in his lap, looking out the window. The sun rose higher and higher, time going by wasted on a man, he lamented, whom he could no longer understand, and from whom he would never again receive understanding.

It dawned on him that his father might be wanting something from his dresser, so Tucker got up and tried to figure out what it could be. He picked up various items for his dad to either agree or disagree over until, again frustrated with the whole ordeal, he spotted in the bottom drawer a vaguely reminiscent black box. He lifted it out of the drawer. Lo and behold, he discovered what his father wanted. Sitting down on the edge of the bed, he opened it carefully and saw many, familiar scraps of paper, notes, and poetry. What this had to do with anything, he soon found out. Amongst all his father's scribbled notes, those in another hand stood out, signed, "Charity." Tucker forgot about them. They held no meaning for him as a boy, because he associated her only as Sylvia's mother or, sometimes, Mrs. Cadwallader. Since his remembrance of having found the two together in bed, he needed no explanation for the notes he now read.

"I miss you, love. See me tonight. Love, Charity."

All the notes were similar, no dates or any indication of which came first, except one and Tucker froze, not having known the history behind Sylvia's mother's death.

"I told Justice. She warned me about getting pregnant. I'm worried." This one was signed, "C.C."

Tucker noticed many were signed this way and he suddenly remembered the note he picked up off of Forty's living room floor. He closed up the box and set it back in the drawer, eager to get going. His father grabbed his shirt and tried to pull him back.

"Wait."

Tucker heard it clearly and slowly sat back down, no less struck with amazement than if Sylvia walked right into the room. After much difficulty and with Tucker's patient assistance, what his father needed to say, gradually came to be known.

"Don't do what I did. Do what I should have done."

CHAPTER TWENTY-ONE

While Tucker visited his father, Shep dug under the fence at Howard's house and ran back to Sylvia and Forty's. When Howard and Mary noticed the dog was missing, they merely assumed Tucker took it with him. They ate breakfast. Mary gathered the laundry to get the washing done early. She thought she would also do Tucker's laundry, so collected his pants and other clothes from his room. She made it a strict habit to check every pocket before putting anything in the washing machine. Out of this automatic routine, she retrieved from his pants pocket an old, yellowed piece of paper. Checking to see if it should be saved or thrown out, she took it upon herself, as part of her task, to read it.

"I'm pregnant. It's true. What'll we do? I need you, Tucker!"

Mary was alarmed by this discovery. The paper and even the writing appeared to be extremely aged. Was it recent? She worried over it. She strived to dismiss it, telling herself it may be a note her brother-in-law hung onto for many years. Although, she thought it very strange he kept it in his pocket. She knew about his escapades in high school, especially with Sylvia.

Tucker may have thought all these years that no one knew of his afternoon walk home from school with Sylvia but, after all, Aunt Justice knew. At the time, Mary worked at the beauty parlor and Justice Walker was one of her regular customers. Women got to talking, while the beautician either cut, colored, or curled their hair. Justice was no stranger to this habit. Since she never married, she had no husband to complain about, as many of the women did. Sylvia gave her aunt plenty to talk about the day after she came home late from school with that look.

"I about *died!*" Justice was indeed shocked, placing her hand over her heart and pressing it close to her. She continued, "I told myself, 'Justice, you have to do what's right for her,' but just stood there. Well, I thought at first I had seen a ghost. She looked exactly like her mother!" Again, her eyes rolled and her hand pressed against her bosom, for she prepared to tell the worst, "She's no longer a virgin. No man will want her now," and, striking the air before her, said, "thank-goodness, for Fortuitous. He'll do what's right for her. I know I can count on him." To herself, as though many nights had already been spent laying awake, worrying about her niece, she muttered, "She looked exactly like her mother . . . exactly like her mother."

Mary thought the note may have been from the incident Justice Walker believed had occurred. She remembered all too well, while she coiled and pinned and squirted solution over Justice's hair. Sylvia's aunt said more than she deemed appropriate.

"Mary?" Justice continued. "Now, I know you are part of that family, so I'm entrusting you with this mission," as her gloved hand, with finger raised, pointedly instructed Mary, "I need for you to tell your husband—better yet, your father-in-law, to keep that boy away from my Sylvia."

Mary never told Howard or her father-in-law a thing. Instead, she felt sorry for Sylvia that her aunt would go on about her in the most deplorable way. Had she done the right thing back then? Or, should she have done what Justice Walker requested of her? Unable to decide, she began to worry over the whole matter and absentmindedly stuffed all the clothes into the washer, sprinkled in some detergent, closed the lid, and started it up.

She looked out the back window at her husband practicing his golf swing. How could she tell Howard about Tucker and Sylvia now? Definitely not after all these years, though she did not know what else to do. The note burned in her hand like a dirty secret. The longer she held on to it, the more she felt compelled to tell someone. She decided to put it someplace. She pried into Tucker's business long enough, behind his back, no less. Hurrying off to his room, looking over her shoulder, she fretted over where to place it, somewhere where he would find it. Perhaps stuff it back in his pants pocket to be done with it. They were in the wash now and would take time to dry on the clothesline. No, that would not do, she told herself.

Mary struggled with the whole thing, going back and forth in her mind over all the possibilities that would determine her next move. The note could be from anybody, she pointed out to herself, not necessarily from Sylvia. It made more sense to her, the reason he carried it around, that it was not old at all. Combined with the fact he left that morning to pursue her whereabouts, she told herself, the note must really be from Sylvia. Mary could not bear to think about the life of a bachelor, but it dawned on her feminine sensibilities, "Tucker's having an affair with that woman! A married one at that!"

Old or recent no longer mattered. She knew, and even Howard had commented to her the night before, Tucker was in love with Sylvia. He departed that morning to find her wherever she may be. Mary clung to this explanation, secretly being a very romantic woman. She cried watching her love stories on television and thrilled each day her favorite story came on. It was her time, her own, private adventure into the mysterious yearnings of a woman's heart. She would never, ever tell a soul, but she rather enjoyed the fact Tucker playfully dubbed her and her husband, Howard Hughes and Marilyn Monroe.

She tucked the note into her purse and told her husband she had a little errand to run, instructing him to keep an eye on the washer for her while she was out. Having something important to do, she whisked away down the street to tend to the matter as it should have been tended to years ago. First, she went over to the beauty parlor to enlist the aid of a trusted friend.

• • •

Tucker cut through the neighbors' yards to get to Howard and Mary's house, so he missed seeing Mary in the process of carrying out her secret mission. He may not have noticed her anyway, considering his frame of mind. Bearing a heavy burden of responsibility, his father's words weighed heavily on his conscience. "Do what I should have done," but what was that? Tucker supposed his father should have plainly and simply stayed away from Charity Cadwallad—

Tucker impulsively decided to tell Sylvia to her face that he loved her. His date with the pretty young nurse would either have to wait or not happen at all. His date with Destiny was due and he did not want to be late.

Once he entered the back yard, he discovered Shep got out, fairly certain the dog returned to Forty's house, so he let it go for now. More importantly, he needed to ask for his brother's help yet again. They sat together on lawn chairs out in the shady back yard. Howard listened very patiently as Tucker told him everything, about Jim Hart and Sylvia, about their father and Sylvia's mother, all of it. Howard told him he knew about their father's "sneaky business," which were the words he used, in order to maintain his usual sense of propriety. He also pulled out a few stories of his own to share with Tucker. Soon, they laughed over the whole thing. It served to calm Tucker for his arduous and important task ahead.

Working as an insurance salesman, Howard came into contact with all sorts of people. Now, while his clients' personal information demanded confidentiality, he found no reason to prevent him from at least pointing Tucker in the right direction. He also had a car. Before they could leave, Tucker needed to go to his old room where he slept the night before, only telling his brother he needed to gather up his belongings. Once in the bedroom, he began frantically searching for the note, his watch—his clothes! Where did they go?!

Howard told him, Mary probably put them in the wash, adding not to worry about his watch, because she always checked the pockets first. Tucker closed his eyes and wondered when his troubles would end. He checked, neither his watch nor the note could be found, unless—he looked into the small waste basket beneath the table, but . . . nothing. He lifted the lid on the washer and pulled out his dripping pants, checked the pockets and found his watch, ruined! The note he never took the time to read, but seemed important enough for Forty to try and conceal from him, disappeared without a clue. It might have been destroyed in the washing machine, or—he shuddered to think Mary had taken it. What did it say?! He agonized over it, while Mary, note in hand, walked into town, planning to rectify the mistakes of the past.

Howard drove Tucker into the very next town. He pointed out his insurance office on the main drag. He and Mary used to live in a modest house at the edge of town, until his father entered the rest home. He dropped Tucker off at a trailer park, told him to ask around, while he went over to his office for a bit. Tucker, according to his brother's schedule, had one hour. Afterward, he needed to promptly return home or Mary would start to worry.

Tucker thanked his brother. He easily located the park's office in the trailer situated out front. The manager of the trailer park told him which space number belonged to Robert Cadwallader. Tucker walked down one narrow lane after another, circling around and doubling back, until he finally found the correct space number and the trailer which occupied it. The park, slightly neglected in appearance and a bit run-down, looked well-maintained compared to the trailer in which Sylvia's father lived. He thought it to be the most run-down of them all. Long, brown streaks of rust stains ran down its sides, crab grass grew thick beneath and around it. Soon, the manager came walking up from behind, lamenting over the trailer's condition, the overdue rent, and the owner of it, recently reported missing by friends.

"They told me Caddie never missed a card night. They were worried about the sort of company he's been keeping lately." The park manager shook his head, "I hope nothing happened to him." Standing side by side in the hot sun, he ended the conversation, giving one last comment, "He's such a quiet fella. Keeps to himself. Kinda different, but quiet."

Tucker thanked him and sat down on the rusty metal steps of the trailer, while he thought over what to do. Unable to think of anything, except to wait by the road for Howard to return, he resigned himself to a long wait in the hot sun, throwing small rocks and pebbles across the street to pass the time. Eventually, Howard pulled up and Tucker got into the car. He told his brother what he learned about Sylvia's father.

Howard knew what he could do. "Call the hospital. See if he's there. Or, you can call the police to find out if he's been picked up. Then, there's always the morgue—"

At the sound of that word, Tucker flashed a look at Howard and exclaimed, "No, not that!"

Howard shrugged his shoulders, unperturbed at the idea of calling a morgue. "Well, you've gotta start someplace, especially if you want to find someone that's—"

"What?" Tucker quickly defended Sylvia's father.

"Well, Tucker, everybody knew he always went a little heavy on the juice," as his hand lifted an imaginary glass to his lips.

"He's Sylvia's father. Think of how she would feel hearing such a thing."

"All right, all right. So, what do you want to do? It's the weekend, but hospitals are always open." He briefly drummed the steering wheel with his fingertips and glanced at Tucker with a teasing smile on his face, evidently enjoying the situation.

"No."

"What? You're not gonna give up are you? You love her, don't you?"

Tucker flashed him another look, this time of surprise. "What do you know about it?"

"Aw, come on, little brother. It's obvious. Why, you two were quite an item as kids." This time Howard actually guffawed.

Tucker did not find it very amusing. "Let's go home. I've had enough. It's all getting very discouraging. I don't need your teasing, either."

Howard pulled onto the highway and drove off, looking straight ahead at the road, trying his best not to grin and smirk, because he enjoyed having fun for a change. Eventually, he settled down and merely drove them home.

Tucker sat quietly all the while, feeling more pathetic about his feelings for Sylvia than he did after the deputy told him he behaved like a guilty man.

"I-I feel like I've gotten off track, or something. I'm going about things all wrong." He suddenly remembered something. "Wait! Stop!"

Howard immediately pulled off the road and stopped. Tucker sat there, one hand braced against the dashboard, the other against the door as though prepared to jump out. Howard sat waiting and grinning, tickled at the sight.

"Well, now, you aren't going to just sit there like that, are you? What is it?"

Tucker remembered he planned to look for Sylvia. She may have visited the trailer park or had yet to arrive. He could go back and—

"Oh, nothing," and relaxed. "Let's go home."

They continued their drive home in silence. Howard dropped Tucker off at his own house, then went on home, himself. Tucker felt thoroughly defeated. He chose to give the matter some time. Monday, he agreed with his brother, might prove a better time to be conducting a search. If he did not hear anything by then, he promised himself to take action. Until then, he tried to enjoy the rest of the weekend, the last day and a half of his very strange vacation.

CHAPTER TWENTY-TWO

Upon entering his unbearably stuffy and warm house, Tucker immediately opened all the windows. Between the heat and his frustrations, he gave up, no longer wanting to do anything. He sat on the couch with his feet lazily propped on the coffee table, shaking his head. Where Sylvia was concerned he always managed to behave impulsively, without thinking at all. He became seventeen again and she fifteen. All the years, since one brief experience in the woods, all the lost years between then and now, never occurred. It felt insane. He no longer wanted to be driven by such adolescent emotions. The intervening years *did* occur and they were years marked by loneliness and buried yearnings for what was probably never meant to be in the first place.

He slapped his hand through the air and declared, "That's enough of that! I've had it!"

Taking his feet off the coffee table, he bravely stood, resolved to live in the present, prepared to get on with his life. Enough chasing after Sylvia, he concluded. It was a never-ending chase that always left him empty-handed and depressed. No matter if it were a dream of his, a wish, or simply unrequited love, he told himself he no longer cared. Stepping outside and pretending to search the sky for another message, he tried to convince himself that his part in all of Sylvia's life ended the moment he left his father's bedside. All he was asked to do, he further rationalized, involved helping his father unload a very old burden of guilt.

Recalling the nurse with the attractive smile, he grinned and strode back into the house. He wrote a note to himself to call her that evening and invite her over to have Sunday dinner with him. He took the ham out of the freezer to thaw, placing it in the kitchen sink, then happily set to work making sure all was presentable for female company. He planted the tender seedlings he purchased from the nursery, watered them, tidied up around the porch, and surveyed all his work. So much of what he hoped to do never got done, but his accomplishments pleased him. Remembering Shep, he decided to check and see if the dog really did go back to Forty's house, so he set off down the dusty dirt road in that direction.

Shaking his head again and laughing out loud, he said, "I keep going back to that house!"

He wondered what the deputy would do now that Jim was dead. No one came knocking on his door to take him away in handcuffs as a suspect. Tucker assumed the deputy saw no need to do that. Perhaps they cleared him of any wrongdoing, which is what he sincerely hoped had happened.

•   •   •

Shep dug furiously to get out of Howard and Mary's back yard. He could hear his master's voice urging him to return to Sylvia's house. On the porch of her and Forty's house, he sat waiting, thin and tired, when Tucker came walking up to the yard. Happy to see Tucker, he ran up to greet him, panting and whining.

Surprised at the friendly reception, Tucker petted the dog and said, "Okay, okay, Shep. I missed you, too. Now, let's go and find you some food and get you some water. Are you hungry, boy?"

Once again, Tucker took care of Shep. Back in their routine, the dog followed close behind him wherever he went. The doors were locked, but he found a bucket to fill with water. On the back porch, the bag of dog food yet remained where he left it. He put some food in a bowl and, after Shep lapped up a considerable amount of water, he went up onto the porch and ate. Tucker petted him some more, finding it unbelievable that Shep, whom he fed and cared for, belonged to the man who won Sylvia's love and devotion.

A car pulled up and parked out front. Soon, a loud, angry voice and other noises emanated from within the house. The back door was hurriedly unlocked and Forty stomped outside, immediately shouting at Tucker.

"What the hell are you doin' here?!"

"I'm feeding the dog!"

"I thought I told you I didn't want that dog here!"

"I know you did, Forty, but what else am I supposed to do? He keeps coming back here like it was his house!"

Forty hurried back inside. He remembered the gun the officer returned. He hid it where Sylvia would never think to look. Determined to carry out his threat to kill Stewart, he retrieved it and ran back down the stairs and out to the back porch, disappointed to find Tucker was gone. He ran around to the front where he saw Tucker reading a letter. Tucker quickly folded it up.

Forty pointed the gun at him, frantic and wide-eyed with hysteria. He put his other hand out, and demanded, "Give me that letter!"

"Forty! What's gotten into you?!" Tucker advanced toward Forty with his hand out, "Give me the gun!"

"Stay back, Tucker!"

Tucker held his hands up, motioning to Forty to hold on, "All right! All right!"

"Now, give me the letter!"

"Not while you're pointing a gun at me!"

"Give me the letter! I know it's some kind of love letter for my wife! You can't fool me anymore! I know what's been goin' on between you two! I found a note she wrote to you! Jim told me all about it!"

"*What?!*" Tucker was shocked over what he was hearing. It turned into an awful nightmare, this man, Fortuitous Sumner, in his life like a nagging headache. "He lied to you, Forty! He was the one fooling around with your wife, not *me*!"

"No! You're lying. Jim was my friend. He was trying to help me out, like friends are supposed to do."

"Come on, Forty, put that thing down and let's talk this over." Tucker pleaded with Forty, but the crazed man refused to listen.

"No! I'm gonna put an end to this right now!" Crying with his hand shaking, Forty pulled the trigger.

Tucker dropped to the ground, to avoid getting hit. The gun only clicked. The letter fell from his hand, but Forty kept pulling the trigger repeatedly, ignoring the letter where it lay in the dirt and the fact the gun was not even loaded. Tucker got back up and rushed him, grabbing the useless gun and hurling it as far as he could toward the woods. He collapsed onto the porch steps, placing his hands on his head, yelling, "Aaaah!"

Forty stood there blubbering, "I'm sorry, Tucker! I'm sorry! I didn't mean it!"

"Jim lied to you, Forty!" Exasperated, Tucker no longer cared. "I've always loved Sylvia! I won't deny it. But, she never loved me." He pulled a small weed from the base of the steps and flung it aside as he sadly concluded, "Not the way I wanted her to. Jim's dead now, so it doesn't matter anymore," and looked up into Forty's eyes, "that's why his dog's here, because it knows Sylvia. It's waiting for her to come home."

He said it, the heavy load of concrete that weighed on him, all that he could not bear to face. The truth gradually settled in to Tucker's awareness, too exhausted to fend it off anymore.

Forty, with a great deal of effort, plodded over to the porch and, very carefully, having nothing left in him to stand, lowered himself until he sat. He felt as he had when the deputy lectured him about playing detective and getting himself hurt. More ashamed of himself than he could bear, he believed all was lost, his friends, his marriage, his self-respect, everything.

Nothing left for him to lose, he unloaded his own burden by saying, "Before Sylvia and I were married, her aunt made me promise to keep her away from you. She made me swear to it on the bible, like a vow. I felt so important then, especially when she called me 'the Lord's private eye.' I loved Sylvia, but she didn't love me like a wife ought to love her husband. I don't know why she agreed to marry me."

Tucker wearily got up from the porch, leaving the letter where it lay in the dirt, and said, "Goodbye, Forty," and began to walk away.

Forty stood up and shouted after Tucker, "You were my best friend, Tucker! They turned me against you, Jim Hart and Sylvia's aunt! I shouldn't have listened to them!" Tucker kept slowly walking away, so Forty lowered his voice, adding, "I should have trusted you."

Tucker turned around and, walking backward, raised his arms a bit and let them fall, and quietly responded, "Oh, well, Forty. Doesn't matter now." He turned back around to continue heading home, truly through with it all, the past, the mistakes made that could never be unmade, his family's secrets, his regrets, everything.

Forty sat back down on his porch to read the letter. Addressed to Sylvia, the envelope contained the letter and an old note, the very same one Forty found in his house Friday. It convinced him Tucker and his wife were having an affair and she disappeared, because he got her pregnant. He read the letter. It was from Tucker's sister-in-law.

"Dear, Sylvia, I found this note in Tucker's pocket. I didn't want to pry into your business, but it brought up a very old memory for me regarding your aunt." The letter went on to relate the story of Justice Walker asking her to have her husband or father-in-law keep Tucker away from Sylvia. It also mentioned Justice believed Sylvia and Tucker had "relations" one afternoon on the way home from school. Mary wrote, "I don't know if Justice was right, but when I found this note, I felt compelled to do what I should have done on your behalf years ago. I went to visit Tucker's father and showed him the note, hoping he might know more about it. It was so sad, so heartbreaking to see him cry. He told me it was a note your mother wrote for him. He tried his best to tell me he never forgave himself, that your mother's pregnancy and subsequent death was all his fault. I am so sorry.

I feel awful now, I brought such terrible grief to the poor man and dared to pry into your family's past. My brother-in-law, Tucker, loves you. I know you're a married woman and I respect that, but he does love you. I think he always has. I hope someday you can forgive his father and your own. They truly did their best, the best they knew how, and they suffer for what they now know were mistakes." The letter was signed, "Mary Stewart."

Forty went into the house and placed the letter with the note beside the vase, which now contained withered and browned flowers. He laid down on the bed and slept.

• • •

Not having any luck at the trailer park, Sylvia decided to give up her search. She planned to return home until Monday, using the telephone instead to make various calls to track down what might have happened to her father. At the back of her mind, she wondered if she would ever see Andrew again. Remembering what Father Jovial said, and what she now believed, Andrew was a guide sent to aid her, nothing more. Nevertheless, she missed him deeply. She asked the cab driver to take her to the bus station, where she waited until the bus arrived. She sat on a bench in the station with her eyes closed and her head resting against the wall.

Drifting on the wind, came the distant strumming of a guitar and a young man's voice, singing. The bus station, with its rows of brown benches and gray walls, seemed a dismal place, so she went outside to see who was playing the music. With suitcase and purse in her grasp, she stood watching the same group of young people she met on the bus with Andrew. One of the girls ran up to her, smiling, and they greeted one another. Sylvia noticed the girl carried a bible in her hand, held close to her like it was her own treasured book. Asking if they had seen Andrew, they said no, but told her where he lived and gave her his phone number. The girl asked Sylvia to join them, but the bus arrived.

"Sorry," she said, "but I have to go."

Nevertheless, she hesitated, looking back, seeing into the bright sunlight of that peaceful day. She recalled how she felt sitting close to Andrew, the comfort of his touch, and she remembered the shopkeeper, so friendly and welcoming. Without another delay, she quickly boarded the bus, knowing it was time to go home.

CHAPTER TWENTY-THREE

Monday morning, the detective set out from his house with a mental list of people he needed to question relating to Jim Hart's death and Sylvia Sumner's reported disappearance. The medical examiner arrived at the morgue to begin another long week of viewing tragedy upon the faces of Life's victim's. The deputy sat at his desk at the sheriff's substation reading the latest report. Robert Cadwallader, not seen since Wednesday, was reported missing on Friday. The story that small, quirky town told lengthened. Bob became mired in its endlessly dramatic plot.

Tucker awoke with a grin, stretching and yawning. His Sunday dinner date with Eileen showed promise. They made a lunch date for Monday. He looked forward to seeing her again. The nurse managed to win her way into his affections. Forty left to the grocery store to purchase more dog food and other items needed at home. He called Tucker on the phone beforehand to inquire on Freckles' whereabouts. Tucker gave him strict warning not to let Shep follow him.

Sylvia and Forty treated one another with respect, though neither wished to uphold any pretense of marital happiness. The sober fact of their mistaken union weighed down their home's dreary atmosphere. Legal papers for an annulment of their marriage sat in the living room. They were shown to Forty, who avoided reading them. Father Jovial and a lawyer, both counseled Sylvia, acknowledging just cause. Aunt Justice forced her to marry Forty and, furthermore, she committed adultery. An annulment was advisable and in their best interests.

Sylvia read Mary's letter and intended to try again to find her father. Choosing a different set of clothing this time, she began to pack, then recalled she planned to use the telephone. Forty slept on the sofa, so she was unaware of his comings and goings. She expressed mild surprise to see Shep at their house, but when Forty said Jim Hart was found dead, she remained surprised.

Tucker Howard Stewart grew rapidly worse due to the emotional strain he underwent. No one knew he pretended to take his pills. Unable to eat, he grew steadily weaker, showing signs of significant depression. The nursing staff held an informal meeting, informally deciding his family needed to be notified. They knew his son came in on Tuesdays for lunch, but they wanted to prepare the family for any eventualities and telephoned Howard. Immediately driving over to the rest home, he rushed to his father's bedside.

The rest home's youngest staff member, Eileen Price, lost her job that morning. She broke one of their rules of proper conduct by dating a family member of a patient. This agreed-upon term included in their hiring criteria, required each employee's signature upon getting hired. Eileen, hoping to move to a more expensive apartment to be near the man she secretly planned to marry, found herself unemployed.

Andrew returned home after he and Sylvia parted. He thought of her and her story, concerned over how she fared in her search. Her gray eyes held him, along with that fateful leap into the Unknown. It drew him further out into a vast realm of possibilities, reassuring him he would see her again. Not willing to wait for when that came to pass, without another thought, he drove to the place where he first laid eyes on her, at the roadside bus stop. Parked alongside the highway, across from the rest home, and next to the shopping center, he sat in his jeep wondering where to go next.

Eileen appeared, walking from across the road toward him. She wore her nurse's uniform and had been crying. She spotted Andrew, wondering about him, when he looked her way. She became terribly self-conscious. Giving him one last look, she stepped down the embankment toward the shopping center where her mother worked.

Andrew sat in his jeep, at a loss as to his next move, when hunger decided for him. Normally a city dweller, the quiet town appealed to him. He turned down the main street, Edenville Drive. Wandering up and down a few lanes, he spotted Millie's Kitchen and parked out front.

Forty signed the annulment papers and left the house to get himself some breakfast at the diner. He sat down at the counter next to Andrew.

The locals whispered low, while someone said aloud, "Look's like Forty's got company." After all, they were the only long-haired men in town.

After sitting together, finishing their meals, Andrew turned to Forty and asked, "Do you know a woman by the name of Sylvia?"

Forty paused a moment, then answered, "No, I honestly don't," and got up, paid for his food, and walked out.

On his way home, he thought over what he could do once he became a single man again. It occurred to him, he could do anything, and raced down the dirt road, raising a cloud of dust in his wake. He turned on the radio and sang along with the music. It blared and carried through the fields, as he thumped his hands upon the steering wheel to its beat.

•   •   •

At the station, the detective acquired information similar to what the deputy received. Robert Cadwallader had been reported missing the same day as Sylvia Sumner, though he did not yet know she was his daughter. Nevertheless, additional information no one else knew, except himself and the medical examiner, called for his immediate attention. The body of an unidentified man was brought in after Jim Hart on Friday, so he left the station and drove directly to the morgue. He requested the deputy meet him, to save him a trip out to the sheriff's substation. A lot of questions needed answering. First, he asked Bob to look at the man getting wheeled out of the cooler for identification.

"Yeah, that-that's him, all right. Older than I remember him, but that's definitely Robert Cadwallader."

The detective motioned for the examiner to come over and give him the details pertaining to the murder investigation. The case was requested by the detective, because he thought it might be connected to a few other assigned cases he needed to solve. When Cadwallader turned up, he quickly lost interest in Mrs. Sumner's disappearance and Jim Hart's suicide. Nevertheless, his superiors required he demonstrate in his report he conducted and completed a thorough investigation, before they officially determined the case closed.

To save time, he asked a junior detective to question Fortuitous Sumner again, about his missing wife and the gun with which he shot himself. He also asked him to talk to someone at Hart's place of employment, to get a statement from them on record, adding, "I didn't know there were still blacksmith shops and livery stables." A deputy questioned Hart's wife. The copy of the report, in his hand, stated clearly Beth intended to press charges against Sylvia Sumner, whose adulterous actions led to the growing unhappiness of her and her husband's marriage. She added that Mrs. Sumner caused herself and her husband severe emotional distress, driving them to alcoholism, and requested to have her committed to the state mental hospital. The detective absentmindedly set it aside without reading it.

He expected a call to come in soon from the young detective. He hoped to expedite the matter and have Hart's body sent home for burial. The deputy complained his phone was "ringing to wake the dead," so many calls came in. Ever since he notified Hart's closest relatives of his death, they kept calling him, wanting to hold his funeral, asking when his body would be released. The detective reassured him the process moved along as fast as it could, adding, "As long as no more bodies show up."

They grimly smiled at one another, the deputy nodding, "Yeah, well, it's a strange town. I'll tell you that."

Meanwhile, Forty was heading out of town, never to return. He crossed paths with the junior detective, who pulled into the shopping center to use the pay phone, having figured out why he was sent, to save the lead detective's—

"What a waste of time that was," he grumbled.

His senior officer sent him to question Hart's most loyal friend, the blacksmith, who said he disliked strangers "poking their business" in his and his friend's lives. The other person to question, Fortuitous Sumner, was not home. The lead detective told him to wait by the pay phone, telling him he would call him back as soon as he finished at the morgue.

When they finally released Jim's body for burial, a car from the funeral home later arrived and his mother, Candelaria Hart, was notified. While they wheeled him away, the detective talked briefly with the examiner. Bob anxiously paced the floor, rubbing the back of his neck where a headache began to brew. He was feeling the heat, when the detective motioned to him to follow him out of the room, so they could talk out in the hallway.

Meanwhile, other events continued unfolding. Jim's sister, older than he, worked with Mary Stewart at the beauty parlor for many years. Mary considered Rosa Hart, now Rosa Smith, as her nearest and dearest friend and confidant. Mary turned to Rosa on her mission of mercy to deliver the letter to Sylvia's house. While not the town gossip, Rosa had a confidant of her own, a young woman with whom she had gone to school, who also worked with her at the beauty parlor, Dottie McGrew. Now, Dottie was the town gossip. Fortunately, Mary had not told all to Rosa and Rosa did not tell all to Dottie. Enough got said, twisted around in the telling that, by the time it spread around town, the truth was difficult to discern.

When Andrew asked a woman in the cafe if she knew of a Sylvia, and described her, the woman perked up and rattled on about, "Yes, I do know her! You wouldn't believe the scandal. She and Tucker Stewart ran off together! Apparently, it had something to do with another man's death, none other than her own husband's best friend!"

"Her husband?" This changed everything for Andrew. He was stunned! Too disappointed to want to stick around town any longer, he quietly paid for his food and left the diner.

Eileen's plans were uncertain, since she got fired from her job. Unable to go home until her mother was off work, she decided to try and find a ride home. She impulsively set out to walk around town, looking for a certain jeep. She located it right away, parked out front of Millie's Kitchen, suddenly remembering she had a lunch date with Tucker.

"Well," she rationalized, "there's no harm in being friendly. I can always call him later."

She walked up to the cafe the same time as Andrew was leaving. Striking up a conversation with him, she learned what the woman said to Andrew. Equally devastated and disappointed, because Eileen not only lost her job, but her future husband, she cried instead on Andrew's shoulder, and managed to get a ride home in the bargain.

•   •   •

The detective and the deputy had their own issues to work out, specifically concerning the deputy withholding information. The detective struggled to write a satisfactory report on Hart's case. He believed Bob had the answers to his questions.

"All right, Bob. You and I both know there's a connection between Hart and the woman reported missing. Let's have it." He was not going to give the deputy a chance to squeeze out of this one.

"Well . . ." Bob rubbed the back of his neck off and on. "It was common knowledge Mrs. Sumner . . . sort of . . . played around. But, that's all it was. I have no idea why she left town, but I really doubt it had anything to do with Hart killing himself. Why, I bet she doesn't even know yet."

He said all he dared to say, but the detective shook his head and laughed. "You've got to be kidding. C'mon, Bob. I know there's more to it than that."

"All right . . . umm, let's see . . . her father here," as the deputy hooked his thumb back over his shoulder to point toward the other room.

The detective was caught by surprise. "What?! What do mean 'her father?' Cadwallader here is Mrs. Sumner's *father?!* Why didn't you tell me that before?!" Feeling his blood pressure rising, he began shaking his head, walking away momentarily, then back again, rubbing his face, as if beyond frustration, wanting to simply bring some sense back to the situation. He had about enough of this small time deputy and his one-more-year-to-retirement attitude. "Look, okay? Sylvia's . . . *lover?* Is that what you're telling me? He's dead and about to be buried. Now, you're saying her *father* is over there in the other room?! Bob. What's going on in that town? Huh?! And, you'd better tell me *everything!*" He jabbed his finger through the air, pointed right at Bob.

"Well, like I was saying, her father here was quite a drinker, himself. That's a fact, and, well, she was raised by her aunt. That I do know for sure."

The detective laughed in exasperation more than anything and, raising his voice, he said, "Bob! C'mon! You've gotta give me more than that! People this woman knows are droppin' like nobody's business! Next, it'll be her husband!"

Bob stood there in silence.

"Okay." The detective realized, since Hart was on the record as a suicide, that story and Sylvia's part in it he would leave for the gossip columnists. Her father was murdered, which involved serious business. "Why don't you tell me who . . . Now, I mean names of people still living, all right?! Who would know 'why and where' about Mrs. Sumner?"

The deputy caved in, thinking to hell with Tucker Stewart. He was not going to take the heat for him anymore and told the detective, "I think there could be one man I know of, who," and stopped himself before he said, 'had a thing for Sylvia,' but he did say, "name's Tucker Stewart. Works with the newspaper there. Nice fella. Real congenial and helpful. If there's anyone who knows, it would be him. He should be able to answer any of your questions about her." He did it and, immediately, his headache began to subside as the detective patted him on the back and finally—

"Oh, one more thing," began the detective, using this last bit of information with which he hoped to pin down the deputy, "there was a report a couple of months ago. Mrs. Sumner's husband shot himself with an old gun he had found?"

Oh, no. The deputy forgot about that incident. His headache screeched its tires and drove right back up his neck and on over the top of his head straight down to his eyes. It pounded. He tried to think fast, because he did a foolish thing, he realized. He returned a gun to a man whom he witnessed for himself was a disturbed individual and a prescription drug addict.

Weakly, he replied, "Yes, that's true. Quite a while back, though. Sure it wasn't longer than two months?"

The detective figured out the deputy's game and said, "I know you're covering up your favoritism of that out-of-the-way town and its screwy, but lovable citizens." He had Bob now, so asked, "What was he doing out in the alley with it after dark?"

"Well, let's see." The deputy tried to recall everything his report said, but decided he had enough questioning for one day and called the detective's bluff. The detective hated driving and particularly hated small towns. "I think you'll have to ask Fortuitous Sumner. He's quite a detective, himself. You two might have a lot to talk about." He turned around and walked off, grinning, because the detective said not another word.

He immediately called the junior detective, telling him to see if Fortuitous Sumner arrived at home. Wanting to be done with this, the young detective lied and said he ran into Mr. Sumner who told him the deputy sheriff never returned the gun.

By the time the detective further questioned Bob on the matter, he would be able to vouch for that. Once he returned to the substation, he checked to see what he put in his report. Nowhere did it say he returned the gun to Forty. The gun that was more nuisance than of any help to anyone, now lay buried beneath poison oak where no man would venture to search for it and no man, or woman, would care to be reminded it ever existed. Shep found it, dug a hole and dropped it in, burying it for the last time.

CHAPTER TWENTY-FOUR

Tucker's spirits ran high, with a good-morning and a grin for everyone he saw. He looked forward to his first day back at work. Unfortunately, his editor gave him an assignment. He asked Tucker to write about Jim Hart's death and the circumstances surrounding the incident.

"Build it up! Draw in the readers!"

The editor wanted it to be investigative and sensational like the big city newspapers. Left alone at his desk, the bright, cheery mood with which Tucker walked in the door, walked right back out without him. Seated at his desk, he leaned back, rocking his creaking chair, which annoyed everyone else, and tap, tap, tapped his pencil on the top of the desk, staring out the window. He dreaded what he knew the editor expected of him, two things that made him wish he could die, himself, rather than face. They were Jim's house, where he had done himself in, and Jim's wife, Beth.

Tucker sank into a horrible mood after that, forgetting his promise to meet Eileen for lunch. He wanted to treat her to

Millie's Kitchen, where she never ate, praising its famous ham and bean soup, served with a generous wedge of cornbread.

Across the road from the newspaper office and down the path one more time, he reluctantly made his way toward Jim's house to begin collecting facts for his investigative piece. The last time he walked there it was cold and rain dripped from the trees. Wind blew cold air in gusts and the day grew dark. This time, a different kind of darkness loomed the closer he got to the house.

Warm air filled the sky that seemed too far away to hear the horns blaring as the golden chariot fulfilled its daily promise. He did not learn of this in school, but from his father. Tucker was not listening to any horns this time or looking for any chariots. Unaware of his surroundings, he walked aimlessly along the path. The green grass he remembered, was curing now and would soon turn a crackling straw-yellow, but it went unnoticed. Grasshoppers clicked and flew across the path once well-worn, becoming overgrown, but he missed it all. His sight turned inward, seeing that which he tried so hard to let go, mostly a woman's yearning gaze and a house with barren walls refusing to reveal the secrets held within.

Sylvia walked this path many times, he thought. He pondered over what troubled her so, that she spent a lifetime running away, always looking over her shoulder. They were the best of friends as children. How did they become as different as night and day? Images of the sun and the moon momentarily appeared in his mind and then drew away.

He neared the ruined house. It appalled him. One of the very first homes built in their small valley, his father told him it had been the finest, with a flower garden the envy of every woman in town. Now, its windows were open like the very eyes of Death, stilled by decay. Ragged curtains hung in shredded disarray, some caught on torn screening laid open to the flies. Weeds, taller than a man, grew thick where once its proud owner carefully tended their beloved home. How many lived in this house? Did children laugh in the fields as grasshoppers skipped and flew one jump ahead? Were any women ever happy within its walls?

Tucker stood, holding a long stem of grass in his hand. He felt deeply for Jim's mother, Candelaria, the pain in his heart unbearably heavy as he ran his fingers along the crisped and sweetened grass stem. Anger subsided into grief, sadness subsided into surrender. He chewed on the stem of grass, like children do, pushing himself to look a little closer at what was unfortunately not the only house Death's dark presence paid a visit.

No light shone the day his mother died. Ever since that day, he feared the dark, reminding him so much of her death. Yet, her death, he knew at last, was as much a part of her life as the day of her birth. Here, at the old, ruined homestead, something different pervaded its surroundings. Life and hope were abandoned along with the house, when Jim Hart sank into his darkest hour. It was unnatural. In its tragic outcome, something hopeful emerged, something yet held in mystery.

In his dazed and meandering state of mind, Tucker unknowingly took the path that led to Jim and Sylvia's rendezvous spot beneath the pines. Once he reached the trees, the needles on their branches prickled his head and arms. He stopped and looked around as though disoriented. The warmth of the trees sweet, perfumed air soon enveloped him, drawing him beneath their sighing boughs. The mystery upon a sudden flow of air through the pines seemed to whisper, "come closer," to step into a world he barely dared enter. He bent down a bit and stepped beneath the limbs, entering a hushed and shaded grove of pines.

"Pine Way," he voiced aloud, remembering the old town of his youth, the activity, the sounds of laughter, and children's voices.

He used to play here with Little Jimmy Hart, and they fought even then. These pines were but scant remnants of a larger grove that existed long ago. Before that, the once-forested valley greeted early settlers, whose descendants built the businesses and homes of Edenville. The discovery of a bygone era quietly existing in the forgotten corners of their valley held him in awe. Yet, he began to feel incredibly sad and weary, for Jim's suffering still lay upon the fragrant, dusty bed of fallen needles. He needed to sit awhile.

Aware no one could see him, he relaxed and leaned back against a sticky tree trunk. Ants in formation marched up and down in their endless trek up toward its height and back down again. The topmost canopy swayed in the breeze. He closed his eyes and silently prayed to God, not knowing who or what that was, even though he attended church every Sunday, all his life. God was only a word, imagining, since his boyhood, a wise old man in the heavens. This morning, he prayed to that which comforted him, and which may yet bring reason to all that happened the past few months.

"Jim is in your care now, Lord. Be easy on him. He never meant anyone any harm. We all have some things we regret, don't we?"

After he stood up, brushed off the seat of his pants, he sighed deeply and thanked God. About to say, "I think I understand now," Sylvia appeared unexpectedly, along with Shep and Freckles, stepping into the trees from the same path he walked.

"Sylvia!"

"Tucker?"

She was about to turn around and leave, but he stopped her, "No, don't go." He felt himself again wanting to take her into his arms, wanting that more than anything.

She opened her mouth to speak, but instead cried. This time, she sought out his embrace, saying, "Oh, Tucker! It's my father! They say he's been killed! Somebody killed him!"

"Your father?! When?!"

She was unable to say.

Tucker held Sylvia, grief rising up within her, not only for her father's death, but for her lover's. The fact of this loss dawned on her the moment she stepped beneath the pines. Jim was not there, because he was dead, but she found Tucker, for whom she had been searching.

Her last phone call, she carried out with great dread to the morgue. In her shock, she hurried out of the house and down the street to find Tucker. Not at home and not at the newspaper office, her hope faltered. In her sadness, she took the path as of old, reminiscing about Jim.

Tucker held her and kissed her hair, soothed her with gentle words, looking at this place where they stood, a sacred . . . meeting place. Sylvia and Jim. Now, he knew. She was supposed to meet Jim here that day, but he showed up, and Beth was angry and Jim was . . . he was so happy to see Tucker, though he never said "hello" to him in years. Tucker distracted Beth from yelling at him, so she turned her wrath on—

Tucker let it go, acknowledging, "He's dead now." He was supposed to be doing a story on him. "Story, be damned," he decided. It would be wrong to drag a man's final hours through the mud of public gossip and judgment. He convinced the editor to drop the idea. In the end, he wrote Jim's obituary.

"James Henry Hart, 33, died in his home Friday afternoon. Born and raised in Edenville, he became the town's hero through his achievements on the high school football team. Captain of the team, he led them on to victory his senior year. He will be remembered by all who knew him. He is survived by his wife, Bethany Hart; his mother, Candelaria Hart; and a sister, Mrs. Rosa Smith. Mass will be held Wednesday, 11:00 a.m., at St. Peter's Catholic Church, followed by a burial at the Community Cemetery."

●

Tucker avoided the shambles Jim created inside his house. He took Sylvia away from there, walking together up the driveway back to the road, arm around each other's waist. Freckles followed alongside, but not Shep. Tucker looked behind and saw the German Shepherd going up onto the porch of the Hart's house and laying down with his head resting on his paws. Tucker felt sorry for him, returning to his master's old house, abandoned by circumstances, sadly loyal to the end. Tucker called out to him. Shep quickly raised his head. He called again and the dog dashed off to join them, receiving their praise and hugs. Together, they walked to Sylvia's house and, seeing she would be all right until he got off work, which would feel to him like an eternity, Tucker returned to the newspaper office.

Once he left, Sylvia thought one more time of Andrew. She stood on the porch, her arms wrapped around one of its roof supports. She watched Tucker walk further away. Not a breath of wind stirred the air. The tall and graceful elms were as still and quiet as a picture in a magazine.

Love, to her, was a puzzling feeling. Both a steadfastness and a fleeting glimpse of heaven, she imagined, a bond between two hearts and an overflowing well for all humanity. The love she felt for Tucker was real, yet not the same as that which she now felt for Andrew. In those places where dreams are nurtured deep within, she slowly grasped its meaning, as immense as the universe and as simple as one moment. She recalled when they lay beside one another in her hotel room. He gazed upon her with those remarkable, golden eyes. In that peaceful moment, she and Andrew began to forge a bond of love. Earlier that day, Friday, when they left the coffee shop, he took her hand in his and, together, they leapt into this great Unknown. For the first time, she saw the freedom always present in her life. Not the kind she felt when she ran to Jim, but the freedom to dream and to make her own choices, to go when and where she pleased, to be *herself,* and to live from *that* instead of the fear her aunt instilled in her.

Sylvia was finally free to be with the one friend she always loved, but had been poisoned and shamed into giving up and losing. All those wasted years, she thought, yet happiness filled her. She marveled at life and the possibilities that lay before her. She felt reassured, knowing that no matter what she decided to do, she and Tucker would always be there for one another. They would always be best friends.

She turned to go into the house, momentarily watching Shep and Freckles dig holes in the yard. She went indoors, immediately spotting the legal form on the coffee table in front of the sofa. Forty's left-handed signature of smeared ink, was upon it. She sat down, staring at it in shock. The seriousness of this step struck her with its finality. Awareness of her father's death was removed from her momentarily. It would return. She carefully folded the piece of paper that meant so much to her, placed it in an envelope, addressed it, pressed a dampened stamp to its corner, and went outside to place it in the mailbox. When she stepped onto the porch into the languid heat of the sun, the dogs ran up to her, barking and whining. She petted them and praised them. They jumped up on her, their paws covered in dirt, her sun dress of white and yellow print now spotted in brown. She tossed a stick across the yard, sending the dogs off to find it. Shading her eyes with one hand, Sylvia laughed loudly and, in that moment, forgot her old life as though it had never been.

CHAPTER TWENTY-FIVE

Aunt Justice made Sylvia pray and beseech God's forgiveness. That one night she attempted to meet Jim, when Beth caught her behind their house, Forty made her pray. He stood over her, holding the bible aloft above her cursed form knelt before him.

Easter Sunday, after she arrived at home, he guided her up the stairs to their bedroom, closing the door. She feared him, what he might do in the darkness of their home. His hands remained placed upon her waist, standing behind her. The warmth of his breath blew lightly upon her skin, his body pressed close to her's. Breathing heavily, he moved his hands downward, outlining her hips, her belly, then further.

"It's been so long, sweetheart. What's a man to do?"

Sylvia's fear immobilized her. Forty behaved strangely. He kissed her along her neck, his breath moist. He removed her hat, her jacket, her blouse, then unzipped her skirt and, when it dropped to the floor, she struggled to hold in her tears.

Within Forty's mind, flashed images of his childhood home. His enraged father grabbed his mother roughly and threw her onto the bed, slamming the door behind. The last thing Forty saw of his father, before his mother's screams began, was the belt, unbuckled and yanked loose by an angry grip. The last he heard of his father, were the words that haunted him ever since.

"Dammit, woman!! Why can't you behave yourself?!"

His mother was not around when his father walked up the drive, home from work in the orchards. He worked ten, sometimes twelve-hour shifts as a labor boss for the fruit pickers, the front of his shirts half-buttoned and soaked in sweat. His hands were big and he smoked big cigars that smelled strong and earthy, like the orchards after they were cultivated, the rotting fruit turned under into the moist, loamy soil. His father seemed larger than Life itself, greater than Truth, and Forty hated him. He hid under his bed, covering his ears until he could stand it no more. His mother cried, pleading for forgiveness. Out the door, he ran and ran, down the orchard rows, the tall weeds smacking his pant legs, their yellow flowers leaving a stain lasting a lifetime.

Sylvia sensed Forty relax as he gently draped her robe around her shoulders. He asked her to kneel. She saw a glint of light upon his face, the spare moonlight shining through the window. She wondered what happened. Something changed in him, his anger subsided, his fearsomeness passed away, and she relaxed, acquiescently kneeling with head bowed. He began to pray.

"Deliver us, oh, Lord, from the hands of Satan that imprisoned our fathers in a terrible grip of fear of Your merciful Light!"

"Deliver us, oh, Lord," Sylvia repeated and Forty continued.

"Bring us to Your eternal Salvation and rip these chains of misery from our hands and feet, so that we might know Your love and Your divine glory! In Your name ... ."

"Amen." They ended the prayer together.

Sylvia stood up and Forty held her in his arms.

"I don't want to be like my father, sweetheart, but what am I to do? You're my wife and I love you. This running around has got to stop. You hear me?"

"Yes, Forty. I hear you."

She finished putting on her robe and her father's work coat over that, before going out to the porch to smoke a cigarette. Forty picked up her clothes. He carefully draped them over the bed frame, placed his bible on the bed, and went downstairs to sit with his wife on the porch. He knew there would be no dinner that night. Settled into their chairs, Sylvia struck a match, its light shining upon her swollen, tear-stained eyes. Within that brief, fiery glow, cast upon her face, Forty saw the man to whom she gave her love. The terror in that moment assaulted him with its truth.

He added a silent prayer, "Forgive me, Lord, for what I must do."

• • •

Tucker continued to ponder that one Easter Sunday, but he eventually learned to be satisfied with the lingering mystery, the unanswered questions. Seeing Sylvia, at times, grow quiet, looking across the road in the direction of Jim's old house, he wanted to ask her what happened.

Sylvia never told him, though she revisited that gray, gloomy day that seemed so far away. She never forgot it. She could not forget the day she escaped to her freedom.

Stealing away from the alley that afternoon, she hurried down the path, intending to meet Jim, as they had planned. The air grew cold, the sun lowering in the horizon. Wind blew in gusts and swept through the pines where she waited for her lover, water droplets landing upon her. She became chilled. She waited, knowing something was wrong, because she never had to wait. He always showed up the moment she arrived. She stepped out of the trees to call for him from outside his bedroom window, but when she approached his house, the window scraped open and there was his wife.

"What do you think you're doing?! You stay away from my husband, you hear me?!"

Seeing that woman's hardened face and hateful glare, Sylvia stopped, put her head down and slowly turned to walk away, back toward the pines. Before she stepped beneath their protective boughs, she saw him, Tucker Stewart, crossing the field and approaching the house. She worried that he saw her. A feeling of intense shame gripped her shoulders, its weighted mark bearing fear and damnation, burning into her bones.

Thoughts ran through her mind. Why was he here? Did he know about her and Jim? She panicked and ducked beneath the trees before he could reach her, but Tucker missed the path she took, so intent he was on the house with the one lit lantern. If he noticed, he would have seen her before she ran off for home, her hand over her mouth where stifled sobs had not a chance to rise. If he noticed, he would have witnessed his past, his dreams crumbling yet again, having left in his heart that which both of them would have yet to overcome.

EPILOGUE

When Tucker was a boy, he once overheard the men talking. They gathered on the porch, their voices low, discussing the war and what it had done to the men who came home. His father did not go to war, listening more intently to one soldier's story than his son, Howard, who had gone. Afterward, Tucker saw his father sit down indoors and write. Once finished, he sat quietly, as though pondering not the words, but the impression the soldier's tale cast into his thoughts. Forgetful, he must have been, Tucker thought, for he merely stood and set aside the slip of paper. He went out to tell Howard he was going back over to the newspaper office to work. Tucker hesitated before touching the piece of paper, for he saw the way his father looked at Howard, an expression of intense fright upon his face, as the soldier, still in uniform, described what he had seen. Reading what his father wrote, the ten-year-old boy was astounded.

"The blasted remains of bodies were only known to be enemies by the shreds of their uniforms that lay like tattered shrouds upon their twisted arms and legs. The images, the heavy, putrid smell of death, the caustic smoke rising from ruined towns, all haunted him."

This was not unlike Robert Cadwallader's experience of the war. It remained a part of his life no one, but those who had been there, would ever know. The only relief from the pain Caddie knew, he found in a bottle of Scotch. He drank until the pain, the suffering agony, went away to that place that jukebox music and dim lights know well.

The last time he saw his beautiful wife, Charity, was on her deathbed, where her eyes looked at his, but never saw, as she passed away and he faded away. His daughter, he saw her last when he put the old house up for sale. A few items, like his wife's jewelry and her personal letters, were all he had to give anymore. He never sorted through the letters to see who else wrote to her, but Sylvia did, the day she waited for Beth. Small notes from "T. S.," and one her mother wrote but never sent, returned to her by Mary, told all and, yet, left so much unanswered.

He thought it strange his daughter wanted his coat and his old, beat-up chair, until one day, after he became sober. It dawned on him it was the chair where he held her in his lap and read the funny papers to her every Sunday morning before church. The coat, it smelled of gas stations and the floorboards of old trucks, the smell of a man who worked on cars for a living. When he came home from work, she ran out to meet him.

"Poppy!"

He lifted her up in his arms and carried her as she buried her face into his neck.

"I *love* you, Poppy!"

She squeezed her spindly arms about his neck, while his black, greasy hands held her close, so she would not fall. It was this remembrance, her father's love, toward which Sylvia ran in hope, all the years, as though searching for her own salvation.

She mourned her father deeply, to have only begun to look for him the very day he was found dead. When the full force of her grief wrested itself free from one last clutch of denial, Tucker held her close.

She cried out to him, "I never got to tell him that I love him!"

"He knows you loved him."

"Why didn't I try to find him sooner? Why didn't he ever come to see me? Why?!"

"I don't know, Sylvia."

It was the day of her father's service. She wore a black dress made of pure silk that Tucker bought for her. A small demi-hat with a mesh veil adorned her head. This occasion also called for black gloves and matching shoes that belonged to her mother, as well as an ebony brooch, finishing off the ensemble that conveyed to all she lost someone she dearly loved.

Assembled in front of the church, the casket containing her father carried up to the altar by his brothers and their sons, they waited outside for Howard to arrive. When he pulled up in his car with Mary, Tucker saw someone else in the back seat, wondering who it could be. So many people attended who knew Sylvia's father. Even the deputy made an appearance, nonchalantly taking Tucker aside, giving him a heads-up that the detective might be paying him a visit. Tucker had enough on his mind and dismissed the deputy's nervous whisperings.

He had nothing to fear. The detective was reprimanded for his incompetency and forced to take time off work. The case concerning Jim Hart's death was closed. His house mysteriously burned down, left unguarded. Furthermore, they assigned someone else to the Robert Cadwallader murder investigation, about which the detective refused to divulge any information.

Tucker watched closely as Howard stepped around to the back of the car and opened the trunk. He saw his brother take out a folded wheelchair, unfold it, and set it down beside the car. He helped a man get out and sit in the wheelchair. Wheeling him up the walkway toward the crowd, Tucker immediately called out, "Dad!"

Tucker's father, the man who did not go to war, yet fought a battle within his soul every day since, recovered from his recent crisis. Tucker ran to his side and proudly joined them, as Howard brought their father, Tucker Howard Stewart, to Robert Cadwallader's funeral. Mary greeted Sylvia, hugging her for a long while. Sylvia thanked her. They talked briefly with one another, until Tucker approached and placed his arm around Sylvia's waist.

He whispered, "I love you."

Together, they walked into the church. He felt her falter once and drew her close to him. In this way, they continued walking up the aisle, Tucker giving Sylvia the strength to finally face her father, so she could, at last, set him free.

THE END

NOTE FROM THE AUTHOR

Word-of-mouth is crucial for any author to succeed. If you enjoyed the book, please leave a review online—anywhere you are able. Even if it's just a sentence or two. It would make all the difference and would be very much appreciated.

Thanks!
Corrine

ABOUT THE AUTHOR

Raised in a rural community, Corrine Ardoin values the friendships and sense of community that exists in small towns. With a creative spirit, she has embraced music, poetry, art, gardening, and storytelling. Her non-fiction book, *A Natural History of the Nipomo Mesa Region*, was well-received. *Fathers of Edenville* is her first novel. She lives in California with her husband, Dan, and enjoys keeping in touch with her two, grown sons and her three grandchildren.

Thank you so much for reading one of our **Literary Fiction** novels.

If you enjoyed our book, please check out our recommended for your next great read!

The Five Wishes by Mr. Murray McBride by Joe Siple

2018 Maxy Award "Book of the Year"

"A sweet...tale of human connection...will feel familiar to fans of Hallmark movies." *-KIRKUS REVIEWS*

"An emotional story that will leave readers meditating on the life-saving magic of kindness." *-Indie Reader*